WICKED HOT

Copyright 2021 Tess Summers

Published: 2021
Published by Seasons Press LLC.
Copyright © 2021, Tess Summers.
ISBN: 9798780985273
Edited by Marla Selkow Esposito, Proofingstyle, Inc.
Cover by OliviaProDesign.
All rights reserved. No part of this publication may be reproduced, stored in a retrieval system, or transmitted in any form or by any means, electronic, mechanical, recording, or otherwise, without the prior written permission of the author, except in the case of brief quotations within critical reviews and otherwise as permitted by copyright law.

This is a work of fiction. The characters, incidents and dialogues in this book are of the author's imagination and are not to be construed as real. Any resemblance to actual events or persons, living or dead, is completely coincidental.

This book is for mature readers. It contains sexually explicit scenes and graphic language that may be considered offensive by some.

All sexually active characters in this work are eighteen years of age or older.

Blurb

Vengeance never tasted as sweet as it did on Hope Ericson's skin.

Sleeping with his rival's wife was an opportunity Dr. Evan Lacroix couldn't refuse.

Except, it turned out, she wasn't his wife—she was his sister.

Oh, the irony. It made it that much sweeter.

Unfortunately, when Hope realized his intentions, she didn't appreciate being a pawn in his game, and the sassy spitfire turned the tables on him.

Evan never saw it coming.

And now he needs to decide which is more important—love or revenge.

This isn't a book about enemies *to* lovers. It's about enemies with benefits—until the line between enemy and lover gets blurred.

THE PLAYBOY AND THE SWAT PRINCESS

BookHip.com/SNGBXD Sign up here to receive my weekly newsletter, and get your free book, exclusively for newsletter subscribers!

She's a badass SWAT rookie, and he's a playboy SWAT captain... who's taming who?

Maddie Monroe

Three things you should not do when you're a rookie, and the only female on the SDPD SWAT Team... 1) Take your hazing personally, 2) Let them see you sweat, and 3) Fall for your captain.

Especially, when your captain is the biggest playboy on the entire police force.

I've managed to follow rules one and two with no problem, but the third one I'm having a little more trouble with. Every time he smiles that sinful smile or folds his muscular arms when explaining a new technique or walks through the station full of swagger.... All I can think about is how I'd like to give him my V-card, giftwrapped with a big red bow on it, which is such a bad idea because out of Rules One, Two, and Three, breaking the third one is a sure-fire way to get me kicked off the team and writing parking tickets for the rest of my career.

Apparently my heart—and other body parts—didn't get the memo.

Craig Baxter

The first time I noticed Maddie Monroe, she was wet and covered in soapy suds as she washed SWAT's armored truck as part of her hazing ritual. I've been hard for her ever since.

I can't sleep with a subordinate—it would be career suicide, and I've worked too damn hard to get where I am today. Come to think of it, so has she, and she'd probably have a lot more to lose.

So, nope, not messing around with Maddie Monroe. There are plenty of women for me to choose from who don't work for me.

Apparently my heart—and other body parts—didn't get the memo.

Can two hearts—and other body parts—overcome missed memos and find a way to be together without career-ending consequences?

TABLE OF CONTENTS

Blurb iii
The Playboy and the SWAT Princess iv
Table of Contents vi
Prologue 1
Chapter One 9
Chapter Two 12
Chapter Three 14
Chapter Four 22
Chapter Five 34
Chapter Six 42
Chapter Seven 49
Chapter Eight 56
Chapter Nine 63
Chapter Ten 73
Chapter Eleven 80
Chapter Twelve 83
Chapter Thirteen 87
Chapter Fourteen 95
Chapter Fifteen 102
Chapter Sixteen 104
Chapter Seventeen 115
Chapter Eighteen 120
Chapter Nineteen 127
Chapter Twenty 134
Chapter Twenty-One 137
Chapter Twenty-Two 145

Chapter Twenty-Three	149
Chapter Twenty-Four	155
Chapter Twenty-Five	159
Chapter Twenty-Six	164
Chapter Twenty-Seven	167
Chapter Twenty-Eight	177
Chapter Twenty-Nine	180
Chapter Thirty	188
Chapter Thirty-One	196
Chapter Thirty-Two	206
Chapter Thirty-Three	212
Chapter Thirty-Four	220
Chapter Thirty-Five	227
Chapter Thirty-Six	233
Chapter Thirty-Seven	236
Chapter Thirty-Eight	240
Chapter Thirty-Nine	245
Chapter Forty	248
Chapter Forty-One	250
Chapter Forty-Two	256
Chapter Forty-Three	266
Chapter Forty-Four	272
Chapter Forty-Five	280
Chapter Forty-Six	284
Chapter Forty-Seven	291
Chapter Forty-Eight	297
Chapter Forty-Nine	305
Chapter Fifty	309

Epilogue 318
Wicked Hot Baby Daddy 321
Wicked Hot Silver Fox 322
Wicked Hot Doctor..323
Thank you..324
Acknowledgments 325
San Diego Social Scene..326
Agents of Ensenada..327
About the Author... 328
Contact Me! 328

WICKED HOT MEDICINE BOSTON'S ELITE

Prologue

Evan

As much as he hated early morning meetings, he was glad he'd made this one. The video playing on the screen in the hospital administrative conference room was mesmerizing; the technology being shown would be life-altering for patients who were missing hands or fingers, and he began making a list in his head of all the patients he'd treated that this would immediately help.

The lights came up and the doctors around the table began murmuring. When the chief of staff, Dr. Parker Preston, finally stepped in front of everyone, questions started being lobbed at him.

"How long until this technology is fully developed?"

Parker smiled. "My understanding is that it's already developed."

Evan spoke up. "So, does this mean it's coming to Boston General? Or is this something that we'll have to send patients elsewhere for them to take advantage of it?"

"The board is doing everything in its power to make this a reality in-house. We want to be an industry leader with this."

That caused another murmur in the group, and people fired more questions at once.

"Does that mean we're going to expand our prosthetics department?"

"Are we equipped to handle something like this?"

"Where's the funding going to come from?"

Dr. Preston made a motion with his hands, like he was pushing down the noise, and waited for everyone's attention before answering the questions peppered at him. "We're in negotiations to bring the woman who holds the prototype patent on the prosthetic. Armstrong Labs' design team has been working with her to marry their technology with her prosthetic. So, the plan would be to expand our prosthetics department and become an industry leader."

"How can she hold a patent?" Evan asked. Companies invest millions—billions—of dollars on research and development in order to hold patents.

Parker grinned. "Because she created the original model in her garage when she was volunteering with the Wounded Warrior Project."

Holy shit.

"There's got to be a ton of places courting her. What makes you think we've got a shot?" someone asked with a laugh.

The chief of staff looked like he was the cat who ate the canary. "We have an in through our ER director. He did some convincing when he went to California to visit family last month. It looks promising; she's coming today to meet with the board, and I'm hoping she'll sign on the dotted line before she leaves."

Whoops and hollers went up as people patted Steven Ericson on the back. He just grinned as people gave him credit for scoring such a great hire.

"I told her she could live with me, and I'd make her breakfast for a year."

Oh, fuck that. That smug son of a bitch is going to bring his girlfriend here?

Evan's eyes immediately went to Olivia across the conference room table. Her face showed no emotion at the mention of Steven Ericson or his role in bringing the woman who developed the prosthetic to Boston General. His twin sister should have been a professional poker player instead of an ob-gyn—her face remained completely neutral. But then, if she'd had, Evan would have had a harder time getting through med school without the constant competition between them. She'd pushed him to do better as they vied for the top spot in their class. Their parents were thankful when he chose emergency medicine and she chose obstetrics and gynecology—thinking maybe having different specialties would lessen the rivalry between the two. Then they were both hired at Boston General and that theory was quashed all to hell.

Their mother had sighed when he told her the news with a big grin. "I swear to God, Evan, you're going to kill me," then called to their father, "Jack, you should have put a stop to this competitiveness when they were eight! I told you this would happen!"

Their father glanced at his wife over his reading glasses. "What would happen? That our kids would become successful doctors?" He looked back down at his tablet and grumbled, "Yes, Judy. I should have listened to you, and maybe this terrible tragedy could have been averted."

"Would you rather me move across the country, Mother?"

Realizing her two children practicing in Boston meant they would both remain near her, their mom suddenly didn't seem to mind their competitive spirit as much. She was almost grateful now that she was going to be a grandma in four and a half months.

But competing with his sister had been the last thing on Evan's mind lately. Although Olivia had warned him to stay out of her business, he was still itching for an opportunity to punch that fucker Ericson in the face. Which would be a problem, since the guy was his boss.

Evan stole another glance at his twin—he no longer gave a shit about how great the potential for the hospital was by bringing the woman with the patent on board. Cedars-Sinai had a great prosthetics department—this would be a terrific addition for them. He'd be perfectly happy referring patients there. Maybe Cedars would take asshole Ericson in the process. But the way the chief of staff was walking around with his chest puffed out—Evan had a feeling her coming here was already a done deal. Today was just a formality.

Everyone stood, and he jogged to catch up with Olivia, who was walking out the door.

"You okay?"

She tilted her head. "Yeah, why?"

"Just..." What was the point of bringing it up? She'd told him she wasn't going to talk about it anymore. "Just wanted to make sure you're feeling okay," he said with as natural a smile as he could muster while putting his hand on her baby bump. "Is my nephew still keeping you up at night?"

"Your *niece* has finally been letting me get some sleep." She paused with a smirk. "I guess it could be your nephew. We'll know for sure around Halloween."

Olivia had decided not to find out the sex of her baby, which was driving their mother crazy. Judy Lacroix wanted to shop for her future grandchild, so she'd tasked Evan to change his twin's mind. Evan knew the possibility of that was nil, so the best he could do was lightly pester her.

They walked down the hall, nodding at people they knew as they did.

"That's good; I was worried for a while—the bags under your eyes were *bad*."

She smacked his stomach. "No, they weren't."

He laughed and pulled her in for a side hug as they reached the bank of elevators. "You're right. You're more beautiful than ever; you've got the pregnancy glow." She eyed him suspiciously as she pushed the elevator call button for up. He pushed the down button, coughed into his fist, then continued, "You know... it'd be easier for me to buy your shower gift if I knew if I were having a niece or nephew."

"Well, since my shower isn't for a few months, you'll have time to find something suitable for either. Besides, I thought that was the point of me registering at Target and Amazon. Mom insisted I do that this weekend."

Evan grinned as the elevator doors opened for *down* and he stepped in the car. "Have fun with that."

She rolled her eyes. "I'll be sure to tell Mom you tried. Talk to you later."

He smiled and winked as the doors closed.

He looked at his watch when the car stopped at the next floor for people to get in. His impatience grew when the elevator stopped again, and yet again. By the time they reached the main floor, the car was full, and he was pressed against the back wall with his hands clenched.

Evan was the last off and ran smack into a blonde woman dressed in a baby blue Chanel suit who was looking at her phone as she tried to walk into the elevator. He wanted to growl and tell her to put her damn phone away and wait a fucking second for everyone to get off, but Preston frowned upon staff being rude to visitors. Instead, he snarled, "*Excuse me.*"

Then his brain caught up with his hands on her toned arms, and he caught a whiff of her perfume just as she looked at him with bright blue eyes that matched her suit. She was fucking stunning.

"Oh, I'm so sorry," she said, her hand on his chest. "I—" She stopped when they made eye contact and she bit her bottom lip.

His ego appreciated that she was as affected as he was by their collision.

With a cocky grin, he looked her up and down, then asked, "You what...? Want to have coffee with me? Take me home with you? Have your way with me in the nearest supply closet?"

Her eyes flashed, then her face transformed into a too-bright smile. It definitely had a hint of a *you wish*; *go fuck yourself,* but she obviously came from good breeding because it almost looked genuine.

"Maybe next time..." She stepped inside the car and pushed the button for her floor. "Have a nice day."

Evan was sure that was debutante code for, *not in a million years*.

He opened his mouth to try another approach just as the doors closed in his face.

His head dropped forward and he let out a groan. God, he could be such an egotistical ass sometimes. Although, in his defense, that line had worked more than once in his favor. And he would have been more than willing to be late to work for fifteen minutes alone with her. But she obviously wasn't a bang in the closet after just meeting someone type. He should have known just by her Chanel suit that he'd have to at least take her to dinner if he wanted breakfast with her the next morning.

Too bad he didn't know where she was headed, otherwise, he'd try to find her so he could "accidentally" run into her and try again with a different tactic. If it was one thing Evan liked, it was a good challenge. Hard to get girls were so much more fun to fuck and ditch the next day.

He glanced at the numbers above the elevator and frowned when the car stopped on the fifth floor—where he'd just come from. That was the administrative floor. Maybe she wasn't getting off there, but rather, someone else was getting on. Did he stand in the lobby like a creeper and try to figure out where the elevator was going next?

Evan shook his head and turned. This was obviously not meant to be.

Like she'd said, *maybe next time.*

CHAPTER ONE

Hope

"I can't believe you're really leaving," her best friend, Yvette, said as she sealed another box of clothes with packing tape.

Hope looked at her friend with a sad smile. "I wish you would come, too. New England is famous for its B and Bs. It'd be the perfect place to open one."

"Yeah, there's just that pesky problem of financing it."

"I already told you, I'll be a silent partner. I need to do something with all the money Boston General is paying me."

Hope had a patent on a revolutionary prosthetic she'd developed in her parents' garage after working as a volunteer with people who'd lost limbs, mostly in combat. Every hospital in the world tried to hire her. It'd been a no-brainer to go to Boston where her brother worked. Still, she'd gulped when the board presented her with their offer. Steven said it was five times what his contract was as their ER director.

"And I told you, money and friends don't mix."

"We'll talk some more after you come on the Fourth." The truth was, Hope wanted her BFF close by, so she didn't care about the money. But she had no doubt investing in a B and B for Yvette to operate would be profitable, so it was a win-win. She just needed to convince her friend to accept her help.

"You forget I've known you since middle school; I know your MO. You think I'll come to Boston, and you'll take me to a few B and Bs that are for sale, and I won't be able to resist."

"I would never!"

That was exactly what she was planning.

"Uh-huh. So, you don't already have reservations when I'm there next month?"

"That's just because I know you'd enjoy it."

"And where we'll be staying isn't for sale?"

"How would I know?"

Because she'd had a realtor looking. Hope was moving to a new city, but instead of having an agent looking for a house for her, she'd had her researching bed-and-breakfasts on the market.

Having a brother with a spare bedroom in a high-end condominium complex had afforded her that luxury. It'd been his idea that she stay with him until she got acclimated to the city, and she happily took him up on it.

Yvette looked at her skeptically and loaded jeans into a new box.

"When do the movers get here?"

Boston General had hired a professional moving company to transport Hope's belongings from San Diego to Boston, but she had wanted to pack her things herself. She wasn't taking much—just her clothes and personal effects; the rest she was donating before she left.

"On Monday."

"So, we have the rest of the weekend. Plenty of time."

Hope narrowed her eyes. "Plenty of time for what?"

Her friend shrugged. "I know you're saving yourself for Dr. Dickhead in Boston, but..."

She interrupted, crying defensively, "I said he was hot—that's all. I already told you, my days of dating assholes are over."

"Yeah, sure." Yvette rolled her eyes. Hope's dating history gave her friend just cause.

"I am!"

"Good, because if they aren't coming until Monday, that means we have time to go this weekend and again this week before you leave on Thursday."

She grinned. "I like the way you think."

"Maybe you'll meet Mr. Wonderful tonight and call the move off."

"Not going to happen. But I'd settle for Mr. Good-in-Bed for the night. Maybe *you'll* meet Mr. Wonderful when you come to Boston next month, then decide to move there."

Yvette pursed her lips and closed the box she'd just filled. "Not likely."

"Never say never."

CHAPTER TWO

Evan

"Dr. Lacroix! Thanks for coming by," Dr. Preston said when he looked up from his computer and saw Evan in the doorway of his office.

"Of course. Although, why you're here on a Sunday is beyond me. You need a life, Chief."

"You're probably right," his boss said with a dismissive laugh before continuing. "Remember the video a few weeks ago in the staff meeting about the cutting-edge prosthetic technology?"

Evan nodded his head, and Parker continued, "We hired the woman who holds the patent."

Biting his tongue so not to disparage Steven Ericson, Evan's boss, to Parker, his even bigger boss, Evan mumbled, "Yeah, I'd heard something about that."

"Good, good. Well, she starts tomorrow, and she's excited to work with patients as soon as possible. And since you see your share of trauma patients who could benefit from her technology... I'd like you to be her mentor doctor."

"Mentor doctor? I see patients when they're first injured. They wouldn't get to her until much later in their recovery. Besides, she isn't a physician, and I have more than my share of residents."

"Maybe *mentor* was the wrong word. I just mean, someone to show her around, be the person she can go to if she has questions about how things work around here. Be a friendly face."

Evan tried to keep his expression neutral. This had to be a joke.

Except it wasn't. Parker had no idea Evan had any animosity toward Ericson, and since Steven was the head of the ER where Evan worked, that was for the best. But be the mentor to the asshole's girlfriend? That might be asking too much.

His boss didn't seem to notice his lack of enthusiasm for the job. "I'm meeting with her at ten tomorrow morning. I'll send her to you by eleven."

He nodded, trying to feign interest, but it was hard. "Okay, yeah. Have her meet me in the doctor's lounge at eleven."

"Evan," Parker said, his tone carrying a warning. Maybe he had noticed Evan's lack of enthusiasm after all. "We were lucky to snag Hope Ericson and her patent. This is going to be huge for the hospital. Make her feel welcome."

Hope *Ericson*? That motherfucker married her?

CHAPTER THREE

Evan

He walked into the cafeteria, still pissed off that Parker had assigned him to babysit Steven Ericson's new wife, so he wasn't paying attention to where he was walking.

"Sorry about that," he grumbled as he glanced at the person he'd bumped into.

It was the blonde from the elevator. She wasn't wearing a Chanel suit today, but rather leggings and a T-shirt, and she was as stunning as ever. *She must have a relative who's a long-term patient that she's here visiting—even on her days off.*

"This seems to be a habit for us," she said with a polite smile. "At least I wasn't the offender this time."

"Nope, I was the one not paying attention. I apologize."

She cocked her head. "What? No supply closet offer this time?"

Evan grimaced. "That was completely out of line. If it makes you feel any better, I've been kicking myself for it ever since. I was a rude asshole."

Her polite smile morphed into a genuine one as they approached the sandwich station. "Yes, you were, and yes, it does make me feel better."

God, she was more fucking beautiful than he remembered. He wanted nothing more than to defile her with his cum all over her face.

"Let me make it up to you and buy you lunch."

"That's very kind of you, but I just stopped by to grab something to go. Maybe some other time?"

Some other time? That didn't seem likely. It felt like serendipity that he'd run into her again. He couldn't let her go now—not yet, anyway.

He found himself blurting out, "How about just coffee then?"

She cocked her head and studied his face. He smiled, hoping he came off as friendly and not creepy.

"I suppose I could take a break and have lunch here instead of at my desk."

"Your desk?" Evan asked as they plucked sandwiches wrapped in cellophane on display and walked toward the dessert station.

"Yes. I technically start tomorrow, but I thought I'd try to get set up today so I can hit the ground running in the morning."

An ominous feeling crept up his spine.

"You start tomorrow? In what department?" *Please say medical records or human resources.* Anything than what he knew she was about to say.

"The prosthetics lab."

Fuck.

"*You're* Hope Ericson?"

A shy smile swept across her lips. "That's me."

No! Anyone but her! Well, so much for fucking her. But he found her interesting enough that he still wanted to have lunch with her. He chalked it up to the idea that maybe he could get some dirt on Ericson, not to mention her invention was genius.

She tucked her hair behind her ear as color crept into her cheeks. Her modesty was almost endearing. Why the fuck was she married to an asshole? He almost asked her exactly that but shut his mouth and let her continue.

"I see my reputation precedes me."

"As it should. The technology you've developed appears to be life-changing."

"I hope so. That was the goal when I was working with wounded veterans."

They reached the cashier, and Evan reached into his pocket. "Allow me."

"Thank you."

He gestured to a table near the window that was out of the way from everyone else, and they sat down.

"Is that what inspired you?"

"Yeah. My family is involved with the fundraising aspect of the Wounded Warrior Project, but I was more interested in being hands-on with the people the organization helps. I started volunteering my junior year in college with the veterans who'd lost limbs in combat. Watching them struggle with their new artificial limbs, I had an idea of how to make them better, so I began tinkering in my parents' garage."

"Were you studying to be a nurse?"

She chuckled. "No. My degree is in mechanical engineering."

He was dumbfounded. "You're a mechanical engineer, by trade, and you developed a prosthetic?"

"I took a course in human anatomy once I became interested," she said sheepishly—almost apologetically. "And I audited a load of classes at Stanford the summer after I graduated from San Diego State. Steven was able to pull some strings, since he's a Stanford alum."

Of course, Asshole Ericson pulled some strings for her.

He found himself hating that he liked her, despite her association with the man he loathed. How that fucker managed to get this intriguing woman to date him, let alone marry him, was beyond Evan.

It wasn't because Steven was a player that pissed Evan off. Being one himself, Evan understood it. Hell, back when they were just coworkers and before Evan vowed to hate Steven Ericson forever, they'd gone out on the prowl together. He'd even thought it was bullshit what Addison Hall had pulled with HR after Steve had fucked her and not been interested in anything more than a one-night stand. Observing that, Evan had been grateful he'd dodged that bullet when the ICU nurse had come on to him and he'd had to work. The comradery between the two ER doctors all came to a screeching halt once Steven did Evan's sister dirty. Evan had tried having a conversation with Olivia about child support, but she shut him down immediately and wouldn't discuss it.

"My relationship with the baby's father, financial or otherwise, isn't any of your business, Evan."

So, he'd shut his mouth and tried like hell to respect her decision to be a single parent without assistance. But finding out Steven married someone else—so soon after finding out about Olivia, was like a slap to his sister's face.

And to add insult to injury, Steve's wife was the woman who'd been in Evan's fantasies whenever he'd jerked off recently. Talk about life's cruel joke. But the way she'd smiled and laughed at Evan's attempt to be witty wasn't lost on him either.

A thought occurred to him. It'd be sweet revenge to fuck that asshole's wife. Even if he and Hope were the only ones who knew. It'd be a secret that would keep him sane when all he wanted to do was punch Steven out. Or even better, something he could throw in his face someday.

It didn't help matters that the dick was a great doctor. He'd deserved the promotion to ER director. Evan had only applied for the position out of spite. Now, Steven was his boss and that complicated things. He was surprised his tongue was still attached—he'd bitten it so much over the last few months.

He gave her his best panty-melting grin.

"So, how are you liking Boston so far, Hope Ericson?"

Her eyes darted to his name embroidered on his lab coat. "Other than being propositioned for a romp in the supply closet when I came for an interview, everyone has been really nice, Dr. Evan Lacroix."

He grinned. "What kind of pompous ass would do such a thing? I'm surprised you took the job after that."

"Well, my lease was up and I didn't want to move back in with my parents, so it made sense to take the job and move in with Steve."

"Yeah, I imagine he wouldn't have exactly been happy if you'd turned Parker down."

She shrugged. "He would have gotten over it. And I'm being dramatic; of course, I could have signed a new lease anywhere. But if I'm being honest—moving somewhere new is scary." She twirled her hair around her finger and gave him a slight smile. *She's totally flirting with me.* "It's nice knowing he's looking out for me until I make friends."

Evan wouldn't mind *looking out for her and being her friend—with benefits*. Okay, yeah, what he was plotting was totally against the bro code, but he and Ericson weren't exactly bros. And his wife wasn't exactly acting like she was innocent. Maybe they had an open marriage?

"So, where's your office?"

"Just outside the prosthetics lab."

"Anyone working today?"

"No, just me. That's why I decided to try to move in today."

Evan felt the corners of his mouth turn up. How she responded to his next question would tell him everything he needed to know about how to proceed.

"I'd like to see how much room they gave you. Wanna show it to me?"

****

Hope

She wasn't stupid. She knew exactly why he wanted to see her office. Her dilemma was how much she wanted to show him.

Hope had played dumb when Steven had warned her about Evan Lacroix, a fellow ER doc and, apparently, an asshole. Her brother, in no uncertain terms, had made it known how much he despised the man. She hadn't told him she'd already met him the day she arrived to meet with the board. Or that she thought he was hot. Or that, even though he'd been completely out of line in the elevator, it'd also turned her on.

She hadn't found Mr. Good-in-Bed when she and Yvette had gone out before she left San Diego, and it'd been a while since she'd gotten laid.

No more assholes! the angel on her shoulder reminded her.

But he'd apologized. And he'd been nice at lunch. Shouldn't she give him a second chance? Besides, it wasn't like they had to do anything other than look at her office.

Even Hope knew that was a lie. If they went to her office, she wasn't going to turn this sexy doctor down if he wanted her.

And why should you? You're a grown, single woman with needs.

"I have enough room," she said with a coquettish smile.

Evan grinned as he stood. "Show me, Hope Ericson."

CHAPTER FOUR

Evan

"Why do you keep using my full name?" she asked as she placed her tray in the return area.

"I like the way it rolls off my tongue." He leaned closer. "And I'm curious how other parts of you would taste on my tongue."

If she'd had any doubt about his intention, that should have cleared it up. She could make an excuse, or just flat-out tell him she had work to do, and she'd changed her mind. But she didn't. She just looked at him out of the corner of her eye and kept walking. "I'm this way."

Part of the reason he'd been using her full name was to remind himself of exactly who she was. He was about to fuck his nemesis's wife. It was going to be sweet revenge when he shot his load deep into her cunt.

Hell, maybe he'd seduce her into having a long-term affair right under her husband's nose. Turn the fucker into the laughingstock of the hospital.

She unlocked her office and flicked on the light as she stepped inside. There were lots of boxes piled beside the standard hospital issue cherry desk and credenza and grey rolling chair. The two chairs opposite her desk were full of bags and more boxes. Evan surveyed his options; he might have to fuck her against the wall. But not before he sat her on her desk and ate her pussy right on top of the papers scattered all over it.

He closed the door behind him and turned the lock. This wasn't his first hospital tryst, and he'd learned the hard way to lock the door.

Although, that one had actually turned out okay since the nurse who'd walked in on him and the respiratory therapist had joined in when he'd sarcastically invited her to. He had been bouncing the chick on his dick when the pediatrics nurse walked in and hesitated a few seconds too long to watch.

"Wanna be next? You can sit on my face until it's your turn."

And, the next thing he knew, he had one pussy riding his dick and the other riding his face.

That had been a good day at work.

But not as good as the one he was about to have.

She turned on a lamp next to her desk, then walked over to shut the harsh overhead light off. Evan noticed the pulse in Hope's neck fluttering and narrowed the distance between them.

"Nice office," he said with a smirk as he slipped his hand under the waistband of her yoga pants.

"It will be once I get unpacked."

With no pleasantries, he ran two fingers through her soaked slit.

"Good girl. You're already wet for me." She let out a small whimper as he pushed two digits inside her. "Fuuuuck, you're tight."

Ericson needed to fuck her more, loosen her up.

He-he. Evan would take care of that for him. The thought of sending her back to Steven, stretched out by his dick on a regular basis, made him smile. If she'd let him go bareback so that Evan's cum was leaking out of her pussy as Steven greeted her with a kiss, that'd be even better.

"It's, um, been a while."

What the fuck? If she were his wife, he'd be doing her morning and night.

Or maybe not. Maybe her appeal was because of who she was and what fucking her would represent.

"Do you want to stop?"

"No!"

Evan dropped to his knees, tugged one leg of her yoga pants down and lifted her bare leg onto his shoulder so her glistening center was in perfect alignment with his mouth.

He wasted no time diving his face into her folds as he finger fucked her hard with his middle and ring finger.

"Goddamn, you taste good, Hope Ericson." He growled between flicking his tongue over her clit and sucking on it.

She grasped his shoulders with her body bent forward as he devoured her.

Evan moved his mouth in rhythm with his fingers and felt her body tense around him as her grip on his shoulders tightened. He increased his tempo, murmuring, "Let me taste your cum, baby."

Her breaths came faster, and he felt her juices coat his skin as she let out a long, soft moan.

"Fuck yeah. That's it. All over my face."

He stood and pushed her tits against the wall, dropped his scrubs to his ankles, and ran the tip of his dick along her fluttering seam.

"I'm clean," he whispered in her ear as he rubbed his cock against her clit.

She pushed back against him. "Me too."

He pressed the tip at her entrance. "Are you on anything? Or do you want me to use a condom?"

He wasn't exactly playing fair. It wasn't his proudest moment, but his integrity had gone out the window when he decided to fuck Steven Ericson's wife to get even with him for knocking Evan's sister up and not taking responsibility for it.

"I'm on the pill."

That was the green light he'd needed, and he thrust deep inside until he was balls deep.

Hope rested her face on her hands against the wall and arched her back, so he filled her even fuller.

Evan gripped both her tits in his hands and slowly pulled almost all the way out before slamming back in deep.

"Your pussy is so fucking tight." He grunted through gritted teeth as he restrained himself from jackhammering into her and blowing his load already.

Hope only whimpered in response.

Moving one hand to play with her clit, he squeezed her nipple with the other as he murmured in her ear, "Can you come again, slut?"

Degrading names was always a crap shoot. Women usually loved it or were pissed. The way she just gushed around his dick led him to believe she fell into the former category.

"Yes!"

He moved the hand that had been plucking her nipple up to encircle her throat and squeezed lightly. Not enough to cut her air off, but enough so she understood that she was under his control.

Evan thrust hard as he polished her clit, his hand still around her neck. Her clit was engorged and her pussy was drenched.

Oh yeah. She loves it. Hope obviously liked being dominated, and he was just the man for the job. Evan was going to get Steven Ericson's wife addicted to his dick. The havoc Evan could wreak in Steven's life made him manipulate her clit faster.

"Whose pussy is this?"

"Yours," she responded immediately, with no hesitation.

"Fucking right, mine. Say my name," he nipped her earlobe and growled, "bitch."

It was the *bitch* that sent her over the edge. He just knew it.

"Evvvvvaaannnnn," she cried out as her body shuddered under him.

Goddamn, she was perfect for him. He was going to have a lot of fun using her—right under Steven's nose. Maybe by the time Olivia had her baby, Hope would already have left Steven for him. Of course, then he'd have to dump her, but still...

The humiliation Steven would suffer was going to be so sweet. Almost as sweet as his wife's pussy.

"Take it," he snarled as he fucked her fast and deep until he was emptying himself inside her. "Take it all."

Rope after rope filled her womb, and he held her hips tight until he was done.

Pulling out, he spun her around and pushed her to her knees. "Clean it."

Next time, he was just going to shove his cock in her mouth without preamble, but this time he let her tend to him, which she did—with enthusiasm.

He pulled his dick from her mouth and cupped her chin, tugging her bottom lip with his thumb.

"Good whore."

Hope lightly squeezed his balls before standing, as if to remind him she was only allowing him to debase her with her permission.

"I really enjoyed that," she cooed as she tugged her pants back on.

"Me, too. Hopefully, we can do it again, soon."

She scrunched up her nose and pulled her shirt over her head. "Maybe. We'll have to be careful though. This has to be our little secret. Steven would flip if he knew. What's the story with you two, anyway?"

Of course, she wouldn't know about Olivia. He ignored her question and simply stated, "I agree, our dirty little secret. We wouldn't want your husband to find out."

She furrowed her brows, as if he'd just confused her. "My husband?"

What didn't she understand?

"You're Hope *Ericson*, right? Steven's wife?"

Her eyes got wide, and she took a step back. "You think I'm his *wife*? And you still—?" She gestured back and forth between them.

He hadn't wanted to ruin their affair already, but judging by her reaction, that might be out of his control. So, of course, Evan did what he always did when backed into a corner—he doubled down.

"Fucked you?" he supplied with an arrogant smirk. "Yeah, I did. And you loved every minute of it, sweetheart, so don't pretend you didn't. From the way you responded, you obviously needed it."

"Oh my god. You *are such* an asshole." She clutched her shirt at her chest. "Get out! Don't ever speak to me again. This never happened."

Evan tied his scrubs. "Oh, it happened, sugar tits. And you'll be thinking about it for months, too. I guarantee it.

Don't worry, if you ever want to go for another ride..." He gestured to his junk. "Give me a call. I normally don't do repeats, but I *might* let you hop on again—if you beg nicely."

"You... You... asshole!"

Still smirking, he leaned next to her ear. "I can still taste your cunt on my lips." Then he pulled back so she could watch him dramatically lick the bottom one. "Mmm, so sweet. I wonder if the other doctors will be able to smell you on my breath?" He paused, watching her mouth open and close as if she was struggling to find words to respond to him. "Hold on..." He reached over to wipe the corner of her mouth with his thumb. "You still have some of my cum right... *Ooof.*"

He gasped for breath and doubled over as all the wind was knocked out of him. He wrapped his arms around his middle and clutched his sides while he identified the cause of his discomfort: she'd delivered a hard punch to his stomach.

It was her turn to whisper in his ear as he was bent over. "You breathe a word of this to my brother, or to anyone, and I will make your life a living hell. Do you understand me? And we both know as the new darling of Boston General, I am more than capable."

Evan looked up at her as he struggled to take a breath. "Wait. Your *brother*?"

****

Hope

"Yes, my *brother*, asshole. Did you only sleep with me because you thought I was his wife?"

"No, I had no idea who you were in the elevator, or when I ran into you again in the cafeteria. It was only an added bonus to find out your last name is Ericson."

"You hate my brother so badly that you'd sleep with his wife?"

The fuckstick wasn't even apologetic. "Yep. In a heartbeat."

"Wow. I'll be sure to warn him to keep you away from Whitney."

"Whitney?"

"His new girlfriend."

Evan scowled his disgust. "Unbelievable."

"What is your problem with my brother? He warned me you were—"

"He warned *you* about *me*? That's fucking rich—him warning *his* sister. Too bad he didn't afford me the same courtesy."

"What in the hell are you talking about?"

Just then Evan's phone rang with a loud foghorn tone at the same time the overhead speaker called, *All emergency personnel to the ER, STAT. Code Red. Repeat: all emergency personnel to the ER, STAT. Code Red. This is not a drill.*

"Gotta go, *darling*." He threw the fact that she'd called herself the new hospital darling back in her face.

"Fuck you."

He reached over and tweaked her nipple. "I told you, all you have to do is ask, sugar tits." Then he opened her office door. "Although, after the punch you just socked me with, I'm definitely going to make you beg next time. On your hands and knees."

"In your dreams."

He gave her an evil grin. "Pretend all you want, socialite, but we both know you'd love it."

Without another word, he was gone.

She slumped down into her uncomfortable rolling chair to digest what the hell just happened. After a second of sitting in the squeaky pleather, she leaned forward and scribbled on the Boston General scratchpad on her desk: *Amazon*, then underlined it. Beneath it, she wrote, *new desk chair*.

Hope leaned back and tried again to comprehend how she could have just had sex with such a jerk. The one her brother had already warned her about and she failed to heed.

But holy hell, he had been hot and dirty. And his dominance... oh, damn. He was right—she was going to be thinking about it for months.

And, of course, he'd turned out to be an asshole. She was like a magnet for assholes, and they were her weakness. Her shrink said it was because she equated jerks with how she liked to be treated in the bedroom.

Dr. Baker had told her, "You can find a respectful man who will disrespect you in the bedroom, you know. You just need to demand both."

That hadn't been Hope's experience, however. The men she'd dated had either been super nice guys—in and out of the bedroom, or pricks—in and out of bed. There was no mixing and matching.

"You need to establish trust and tell your partner what you want."

She'd tried that, and freaked out the poor, kind and caring accountant she'd been dating.

"You want me to do what?" he'd asked, horrified when she told him to call her a slut and push her head down on his cock.

Conversely, the aggressive guy who liked to choke her also liked treating her like shit when their clothes were on.

There was no winning. So, she settled for one-night stands with assholes for the sex, and her friendships for intimate relationships.

Evan Lacroix would be no different. Maybe she would even beg him sometime; if she were desperate enough, and she felt he could keep a secret.

Hope had a feeling, however, there would be no discretion on his part. He'd use sleeping with her as a way to get to her brother.

She had no idea why the two men hated each other so much, but there was no way she'd allow someone to use her to hurt someone she loved.

She'd just have to find a different asshole to use her for sex. He shouldn't be too hard to find.

The voice over the loudspeaker kept calling for emergency room personnel. Obviously, something big had happened, and her brother was out of town with Whitney. If he knew she was at the hospital, he'd expect her to help out if she could. Plus, Hope wanted to start her career at Boston General with a good impression that she was a team player.

She wasn't a trained medical professional, but she could transport patients from the ER to x-ray or surgery, run errands, or assist as needed. She knew she could be useful, so after stopping in the bathroom to wipe the remnants of Dr. Dick's cum from between her legs, she followed the signs to the emergency room.

CHAPTER FIVE

Evan

It was the calm before the storm—sort of. The ER staff was darting around, prepping for victims from a passenger train crash. Even Parker was in the ER, relaying what the personnel on scene were telling him to the hospital staff.

He'd also been on the phone with Dr. Ericson. And, of course, the asshole was cutting his vacation short to show up and save the day.

Evan knew if he didn't hate him, he'd respect that Steve was dropping everything and coming to help when his department needed it. That's what a good leader did. But, since he loathed the man, he'd rather view it as Dr. Ericson feeding his ego. Like, they couldn't function without him.

The corner of Evan's mouth turned up at the thought of what he'd just done to the man's sister. And what he was going to do to her in the future. Because there was going to be a repeat—he'd bet his Mercedes she'd be back for more.

She'd been fucking perfect—sassy and smart, then submissive when he wanted her to be. At first, he'd been disappointed it hadn't been Steven's wife that he'd fucked, but now that he'd had some time to think about it, the sister angle might even be better. If only Hope wasn't on birth control. Knocking her up would be the sweetest revenge of all.

Except there'd be no way he could ignore if he had a baby. How Steve could act like becoming a father meant nothing was beyond Evan.

He heard Parker's deep voice coming from an empty office around the corner from his closet-sized one—it was nothing like the new darling of Boston General's.

"Hope! I didn't know you were here. I was just talking to your brother. He's on his way."

"I'm here to help in any way you need me. I'm sure I can be of some use, somehow."

Oh, little socialite, don't tease me, Evan thought with an internal groan. Yeah, he'd just cum inside her thirty minutes ago, but he had a feeling he could be insatiable when it came to getting naked with Hope Ericson.

He wasn't sure he'd be able to wait for her to come to him, begging.

"The staff are prepping rooms with supplies until the first victims get here; I'm sure your help would be appreciated."

That was Evan's cue. He rounded the corner into the makeshift command center Parker had created.

"Hey, Dr. Preston, could I get some help..." He stopped short, like he hadn't realized there was someone in the office with Parker.

"Oh, hi." He stuck his hand out to Hope. "Evan Lacroix."

She eyed him suspiciously and shook his hand. "Hope Ericson."

"You're Hope Ericson?" He looked over at Parker. "The woman you told me about?"

The chief of staff was beaming. "While I'm not thrilled with the circumstances, I'm glad you two are able to meet now since I suspect tomorrow's agenda might go out the window. Hope, I asked Evan to be your mentor doctor. Show you around, introduce you to everyone, be the person you can go to if you have questions."

Evan tried to hide his smirk as a blush crept up her chest. "Oh, Dr. Preston, that's very considerate of you, but I have Steven to help show me the ropes. Besides, I'm sure Dr. Lacroix has better things to do with his time than babysit me."

Babysit. That was exactly how Evan had considered the assignment when Preston first told him about it.

"It's no trouble at all, Hope. I'd be honored to be your go-to guy."

He noticed her swallow hard as Parker spoke up. "I know you have Steven, but I think for the sake of appearances, it'd be better if you had someone else other than your brother help you out. I thought since you and Evan will be working together in the future with trauma patients, he'd be a good fit."

She turned her back to where Parker was seated and glared at Evan, mouthing, *you asshole,* then morphed into a bright, fake smile before she turned back to their boss.

"Of course, I wasn't thinking about how it'd look if I were going to my brother with questions. As long as Dr. Lacroix doesn't mind me *bothering* him."

There was a warning with her use of the word *bothering*, and if he'd been a smarter man, he would have recognized it. But he was feeling too cocky to take notice.

"Great, now that that's settled, I could use some help stocking the trauma rooms. Come on, I'll show you where the supply closet is."

Evan knew there was a twinkle in his eye as he walked out, and he hoped like hell his big boss didn't notice it. He heard Parker say, "I appreciate you stepping up to help. You're in good hands with Evan. He'll show you what to do next."

Oh, if the chief only knew how good of hands or what he wanted to show her.

****

Hope

She fought to keep her face neutral when the chief of staff told her she was in good hands with Evan. The man had just had those "good hands" around her throat and on her clit.

"Right this way," the asshole said smugly when she walked out of the office.

She wanted to smack the arrogant look right off his face. Instead, she plastered on a polite smile as they walked through the halls.

He flashed his badge in front of a card reader and a lock clicked just as he pushed on a door. A bright fluorescent light came on automatically as he stepped inside. Evan held the door for her, and she crossed her arms at her chest, not budging from where she stood in the hall.

"I'll wait out here. You seem to have a thing for supply closets."

"While I wouldn't mind being balls deep in you again," he drawled as if she amused him, "we don't have time. And I already told you, you're going to have to beg me first. But, right now, I do need an extra set of hands so, you're safe—this time."

Hope rolled her eyes and walked into the small space. Evan moved away from the door and it closed automatically.

He stood behind her and reached past her with one hand toward a box on a high shelf. "We'll need these." With his other hand, he groped her boob over her shirt.

She turned to glare at him.

"They're just so irresistible," he said with a grin.

"The supply closet just brings it out in you?"

"Hardly, socialite. More like, you do."

"Even if I'm not your competition's wife? What's the fun in that?"

"Oh, it was *very* fun, sweetheart. You can't deny it. And Steven is hardly my competition."

"What is the deal with you two?"

"Ask your brother."

"I'm asking you."

He plucked boxes of gauze from the shelf behind her and piled them in her hands.

"Not my story to tell."

"But—"

His phone rang with the same obnoxious ringtone it'd had in her office.

"Time to go, darling."

It was like a mask slipped on his face, and his expression became serious while he grabbed a few more white boxes with black lettering, then walked out behind her.

They reached the nurse's station, and he dropped the boxes on the desk before washing his hands in a nearby sink while telling her, "You can set those there, then try to stay out of the way."

"Are you always this charming?"

He winked as he dried his hands, then pulled a pair of blue gloves. "No. Usually I'm an asshole." Then, without another word, he jogged toward the entrance.

Seconds later, he had his stethoscope in his ears, listening to a patient's heart as he ran alongside a gurney through the ER doors and fired off orders to waiting nurses, then headed back outside again. The scene was controlled chaos—the flurry of moving people seemed to know exactly where they were going, and Evan's command of the scene was sexy as fuck.

Hope noticed her brother come through the doors with a patient, then bark out orders, just like Evan had. Watching the team of doctors move the incoming crash victims was mesmerizing. Even Parker was bringing patients through the door.

"Hope, can you take this patient to x-ray?" Evan called to her. She'd been leaning against the wall, trying to do as he'd said—stay out of the way, but now it seemed she could be useful.

She pushed off the wall and hurried forward. "Of course."

Her brother must have heard Evan say her name, because he looked in her direction and smiled as if he'd just noticed her.

"Hey, sis. Thanks for helping."

"Glad I can do something."

When she returned to the ER, all the train victims had been moved inside and the doctors were working on the most critical. Nurses were moving back and forth between patients and there was a line of gurneys waiting to be transported to x-ray. She pushed the gurney of the next patient that was ready and brought back one. She continued this for over an hour until everyone needing x-rays had them and had been returned to the ER.

She caught a glimpse of Evan and her brother moving between rooms—their expressions serious. Hope had a newfound respect for her brother—which was saying a lot because she had already thought he was amazing. And Dr. Dick had only grown more appealing.

Dammit.

Doesn't matter—I'm staying away from him. He's not going to use me to hurt my brother.

She'd just have to make do with the memory of their time in her office until she found another asshole to have dirty sex with.

But she had to admit, the sex with Evan was going to be hard to beat.

Chapter Six

Evan

He'd watched Hope transport patients and do anything asked of her without complaint. Her blonde hair that she'd had pulled up into a high ponytail had loose strands, and her cheeks were flushed from how much energy she'd been exerting.

Seeing her like that only made him want to fuck her again. Her pitching in when she wasn't even technically on the payroll yet was sexy as hell. *She* was sexy as hell—period.

He hadn't lied when he'd told her he didn't do repeats. That led to misunderstandings about his intentions, which were simple: he wasn't looking for a relationship. He was only interested in a good time, one time, then he was onto the next woman—or two if he were lucky.

But for Hope, he'd make an exception. And he might not even make her beg. At least beforehand. But once he got her naked again, she was going to be on her knees pleading for his cock. He'd make sure of it.

It was three in the morning when things had calmed down enough for him to grab an energy bar. He saw Parker talking to Hope at the nurse's stand—her baby blues had dark circles under them and her hair was more of out her ponytail than in.

"Go home," the chief of staff was saying as Evan approached. "We'll reschedule our meeting to Tuesday.

Come in tomorrow only if you feel like it, but not before the afternoon. That's an order."

Evan wished Parker would order him to stay home, but there was a fat chance of that. They were down an ER doc, and everyone had been working more than their share.

Hope wasn't part of the ER team, and probably wasn't used to running on little sleep. Evan knew Parker wanted her fresh and ready to put Boston General's prosthetics department on the map.

"I'll have Evan plan on showing you around Tuesday at eleven."

"Really, Parker. I'm perfectly capable of introducing myself around."

Evan was about to step forward and quash that, but thankfully their boss replied, "Nonsense."

She didn't argue any further. *Good girl.*

Francisco Valencia, one of the orthopedic surgeons working in the ER tonight, approached and put his hand on Hope's shoulder.

"Thanks for all your help. You are amazing for stepping up like that."

She looked up at the good-looking doctor and smiled. "I didn't do much, but thank you. I was glad I could be of use."

Francisco ran his hand up and down her arm. "We're excited you're here, Hope. I can't wait to work with you."

Okay, Rico Suave, move along.

"I look forward to it."

She lifted her purse strap over her shoulder and walked toward the exit when Francisco said, "Maybe we could have lunch sometime?"

Fuck no, she doesn't want to have lunch with you sometime.

Hope tucked the stray hairs behind her ear. "I'd like that."

Dafuq! You'd like that?

"Great. I'll swing by your office sometime this week."

"I'll see you then."

Yeah, that's not going to work.

Evan approached Hope as she walked toward the sliding doors and possessively placed his hand at the small of her back—hoping the other doctor noticed. Leaning down, he murmured in her ear, "I'm looking forward to our tour on Tuesday. Be sure you're well rested."

"Oh, yes, our tour. I'll be sure to go a few rounds with my punching bag in preparation for it."

He couldn't help but smile at her sass and liked that she stutter-stepped when he dished it back to her as they walked outside. "I'll bring the handcuffs, then."

She recovered quickly. "In your dreams."

"Oh, Hope, darling, that's exactly what I'm going to be dreaming about. How did you know?"

She turned to face him under the amber parking lot lights with her hand on her hip. "Don't you have work to do?"

"Yep. Just need to make sure you get to your car safely and thank you for your help."

"And pee on me in front of Dr. Valencia," she grumbled as she walked toward a group of cars.

Was it bad that he found it sexy that she could see right through him? He jogged to catch up to her.

"I mean, that's not my kink, but if you want me—"

She glared at him. "I should have punched you in the mouth, so it'd have to be wired shut."

"But then I wouldn't be able to use my tongue." He leaned closer. "And you wouldn't want that..."

"You're such a jerk."

He shrugged. "I notice you didn't deny it, and I already told you, I'm an asshole."

"You don't have to keep trying to convince me. I believe you."

The lights of a white Tesla with California plates flashed as she held up her fob.

"Thank you for walking me to my car," she said almost begrudgingly when she opened the driver's side door. "I appreciate it."

"It was my pleasure." Evan fought back the urge to kiss her lips, and instead just stared at them for a moment before murmuring, "Drive safely, Hope Ericson. Sweet dreams."

"Good night, Dr. Lacroix. You were—"

He quirked a brow, waiting for her to finish her thought. She gave him a fake smile, as if she'd decided against whatever she'd been about to say, and instead said, "I'll see you Tuesday," as she slid into the front seat.

"I look forward to it, *darling*."

She shot him a look and closed the door. Evan waited until she started her car and drove off, then with a small shake of his head and a smile, he headed inside.

As much as he'd love to rub it in Steven's face that he'd just fucked his little sister, he decided against it—for now. It'd be much sweeter once she was in love with him, and he'd just dumped her.

****

Hope

She'd almost told Evan that he'd been incredible to watch tonight but thought better of it. His ego was already big enough.

He really had been, though. Hope had seen a whole different side to him as she watched him soothe patients who were hurt and scared while he tended to them with compassion. She had to admit, it'd only made the jerk hotter.

It didn't matter how hot he was. She wasn't going to let Evan use her as a pawn in whatever was going on between him and Steven. She didn't care how nice his dick was.

Francisco had seemed nice. And boring. At least her brother would approve.

With no traffic, she was back at Steven's condo in no time and was surprised that Lola was nowhere to be found.

Hope: Should I be concerned that your dog isn't here?

Her brother replied right away.

Steven: She's with Whitney.

Hope: Okay. Good night. See you tomorrow.

Steven: Thanks again, sis. You really stepped up tonight. Parker hasn't stopped raving about you.

Hope: I knew it's what you'd want me to do.

Steven: Love you. Get some rest. Glad you made it home safe.

She set her alarm for ten and was asleep before her head even hit the pillow. But it wasn't a dreamless slumber. That bastard taunted her, even in her sleep. She dreamed he was delivering her baby, then when she was in the middle of pushing, he left to help another woman in labor—leaving her to have the baby by herself. Except Hope ended up giving birth to a litter of Golden Retriever puppies, and the hospital morphed into a mall, where she went shopping in her hospital gown. While she was shopping, she ran into Evan and a different woman than the one whose baby he'd helped deliver. This one was shopping for a wedding gown, and Steven was the store clerk helping them.

She stared at the ceiling when she woke up, contemplating what the hell her dream was supposed to mean. She had no idea, but suspected it was her subconscious telling her to steer clear of Evan Lacroix.

"Way ahead of you," she murmured out loud as she swung her feet off the bed and headed to the en suite bathroom.

The only problem was, her boss was making that impossible.

Chapter Seven

Hope

Her brother still wasn't home when she left the condo at eleven thirty. How he was able to keep those hours, she had no idea. Eight hours of sleep was a minimum for her. She skated by on six or seven in college but was usually groggy during her first class of the day.

That'd been part of the reason she hadn't pursued medicine like Steven had. She knew there was no way she could function with a doctor's schedule. She'd made it clear in her interviews that she didn't do meetings before ten and that she shouldn't be expected in the lab before then, either. It wasn't that she didn't work hard once she got to work, or that she didn't put her hours in. She'd often found herself still at Armstrong Labs at midnight. Or when she was developing the prototype in her parents' garage, her father would come down at one in the morning and tell her to go to bed.

As she walked through the hospital doors, she found herself wondering if Evan was still working, too. Not that it mattered because she couldn't care less.

The fact that she found herself using her fancy new badge to access doors that led to the emergency wing had nothing to do with that arrogant dick. *Nothing.* She just wanted to see how her brother was doing—that was all.

Dr. Preston was the first face she recognized.

"Oh, Parker, I can't believe you're still here. You must be exhausted."

"We rotated sleep shifts, so I got a couple of hours."

She glanced around and casually asked, "All the doctors? Has anyone been able to go home?"

"A few are getting ready to go. Steven's going to be here for another few hours, at least."

Yes, of course, her brother—that's why she was asking.

"Well, you all are rock stars in my book."

"I've been called a lot of things," came a deep voice from behind her. "But never that. I like the sound of it. I could be a rock star."

Hope didn't even have to turn around to know who it was. Their boss was standing two feet away in front of her, so she couldn't respond with a biting retort. Instead, she plastered her best *fuck you* smile on and turned to face Evan.

"Complete with a guitar and everything?"

"Nah, I'm more of a drums guy."

Parker chuckled. "Glad to see you still have your sense of humor even after twenty-four hours of this place, Evan."

Evan gave a pointed look at Hope. "It's the company."

"Aw, Dr. Lacroix, you're too kind. Although, I think you might be delirious from lack of sleep."

"I'm not going to argue that I don't need sleep. I'm going to call an Uber because I should not be behind the wheel right now."

She found herself saying, "I can give you a ride."

What the hell are you doing, Hope?

He cocked his head and looked at her thoughtfully. "You'd do that for me?"

"I saw you in action last week. Boston General can't afford to lose you in the ER." She glanced at Parker. "From what I understand, you're already down a doctor."

"At least one," Parker corrected. "We could probably stand to add two more on staff, but we're having a problem just finding one."

Evan gave her a genuine smile, the bags under his azure eyes evident. "That's very kind of you to offer, but it makes more sense to take an Uber. I've seen your office—you still have a lot of unpacking to do."

"You've seen her office?" Parker chimed in.

Even exhausted, Evan was fast on his feet. "Just in passing. I was walking by yesterday and noticed."

"Were you the one who peeked their head around the corner when I was sitting on the floor?"

She glanced up at Evan nervously, then over at Parker. She'd always been a terrible liar. The worst of her siblings, by far. They all knew she was the weakest link when it came to hiding things from their parents.

"Nope, wasn't me. Must have been another one of your admirer's."

"Another one" implied that Evan was one. Hope knew that was bullshit.

"Well, I hope you both get some rest. I'm off to make a dent in my boxes. If you see my brother, please tell him to stop by and see me if he gets a chance. I have a feeling, with his new girlfriend, this is the only place I'm going to be seeing him."

A corner of Parker's mouth turned up. "Steven has a girlfriend?"

Evan was visibly scowling, although Parker didn't seem to notice.

Hope fidgeted with her hands in front of her. "I probably shouldn't have said anything. That's his story to tell, not mine."

"Mum's the word," Parker said with a twinkle in his eye.

"Thanks. I'll see you tomorrow," she offered up generically, since she had plans with both men tomorrow.

"Ten a.m.," Parker said with a smile. "Then Evan can show you around at eleven."

"Why don't we meet in the cafeteria instead of the doctor's lounge?" Evan asked. "That way we can grab some coffee and maybe even an early lunch if you're hungry."

She knew he was being pleasant for show in front of their boss. Still, she'd play along.

"Sounds great."

"My treat." Even with the bags under his eyes, his smirk was still annoying. And sexy, dammit.

"That's not necessary."

Since I make way more than you. She didn't add that, of course, but she might have if Parker hadn't been standing there listening to their exchange.

"I insist. My way of welcoming you to Boston General."

Oh, eating my pussy in my office wasn't welcome enough? Again, she didn't say it, but she might have if they'd been alone.

Dammit, I'm wasting all my zingers. Normally, she'd sit, tongue-tied, trying to think of a clever comeback, only to come up with something long after the moment had passed and then she'd obsess over what she should have said.

Her mother had taught her to be gracious, so she simply responded, "That's very kind. Thank you." Maybe she could "accidentally" dump her soda in his lap. Or worse.

Parker guffawed. "Lunch in the cafeteria? Slow down, big spender."

Evan shrugged, unfazed. "Just warming her up to ask her out to dinner later. Maybe Chez Magnifique."

The way Dr. Preston raised one eyebrow, Hope got the impression that the restaurant was a bit swankier than the hospital cafeteria. She couldn't tell if Evan taking her to dinner was something Parker approved of.

She patted his arm. "Now I know you're delirious. Go get some sleep, Dr. Lacroix."

"Thanks again for the offer to drive me home."

"I love how well you're already fitting in here, Hope," Parker said with a smile.

"I better go unpack. I'd like to begin working with patients as soon as possible."

Her boss nodded in approval.

She smiled at the silver fox. "You better get home, too. Your wife is probably wondering where you are."

"Oh, Boston General is Parker's wife," Evan said with a wry laugh.

Parker nodded solemnly. "Sad, but true."

That made her sad. She was all for being dedicated to her job, but she knew there was more to life than just work. She was thrilled her brother had finally seemed to realize that. He appeared to have fallen hard for his attorney lady friend. Parker was too great of a catch to be alone.

"Maybe Steven's girlfriend has a sister," she said with a wink.

Her boss returned the wink with a conspiratorial smile. "Find out for me."

She glanced up to find Evan scowling again, just like he did anytime she mentioned her brother. Steven had had the same reaction when telling her to avoid Evan. "He's an asshole."

She couldn't disagree. A hot asshole, but an asshole, nonetheless. How did the two men manage to work together without going to fisticuffs?

She had two new things to add to her "To Do" list. Right under *unpack office* and *buy new chair*, she was going to include *find Parker a date,* and *uncover the reason for Steven and Evan's feud.*

She obviously had her work cut out for her.

CHAPTER EIGHT

Evan

He woke up with the summer sun rising on Tuesday morning and ran five miles before showering and heading to the hospital with a spring in his step.

For the first time in a long time, he was excited about going to work.

It wasn't that he didn't enjoy his job—he did. What he did was meaningful and fulfilling, but he was never *excited* about going there. Apparently, plotting to get his nemesis's sister to fall in love with him changed that. Who knew revenge could be so motivating? The fact that his enemy's sister was hot, smart, and a great fuck might have also had something to do with it.

He wore a cobalt blue button-down with his favorite tie, an abstract design that looked like a blue and teal flame. His sister had bought it for him—she said it brought out the blue in his eyes. He always received a lot of compliments when he wore it, so he thought it was a good choice. He'd be changing into scrubs when he started his shorter shift in the ER this afternoon, but until then, he'd look good. Distinguished. Worthy of a socialite.

He parked his Mercedes in the staff garage, grabbed his white lab coat from the back seat, and made his way inside the hospital. There were patients he needed to check on and reports he needed to dictate before his meeting with Hope at eleven.

The next time he glanced at his watch, it read twenty-two minutes after eleven.

"Shit," he muttered as he stood abruptly from his desk. He'd been planning on being late; a little powerplay to make her wait for him, but by the time he made it to the cafeteria, he'd be a full thirty minutes late. Even he realized that was pushing it.

Evan didn't exactly power walk to the cafeteria, but he didn't leisurely stroll either. Before he even grabbed a tray, he walked through the area where the food was displayed and into the part where the tables were. Maybe she'd sat down in a booth to wait for him. It was doubtful, but one never knew.

Oh, she was there all right—looking as beautiful as ever in a white sundress with big hot pink flowers as the design. Her hair was curled and loose around her shoulders, and her makeup was expertly done, just like the first day in the elevator.

And sitting next to her laughing was Francisco Valencia.

"Motherfucker," Evan murmured under his breath. That goddamn orthopedic surgeon was going to be a thorn in his side.

He took a deep breath in and stood up taller. He was Evan Lacroix, dammit. Arrogant, hotshot doctor. Valencia was no match for him, and Little Miss Socialite didn't stand a chance now that he'd set his sights on her.

Still, he didn't like seeing the two of them in the booth together, laughing like they were lovers.

He sauntered over to where the two were sitting like he didn't have a care in the world.

Hope noticed him first and shot him a dirty look. "Oh, hi. So nice of you to make it."

"Yeah, sorry about that. I got, um, hung up in the supply closet."

She jerked her head up, and a hurt look flashed across her face, but it was quickly replaced with a pissed off one. That morphed into a look of disinterest and boredom, that Evan was sure only came from years of her debutante training.

"That's okay." She beamed at Francisco and patted the other doctor's hand. "Dr. Valencia came to my rescue." She looked up at Evan with disdain. "He offered to show me around, so you can go. I'm sure you have more supplies to replenish or something."

"No, I'm all set. I got all my supplies taken care of."

She gave him her patented *go fuck yourself* smile. "How wonderful for you. But really, you can go."

He plopped down next to her in the booth and lifted his chin toward Francisco while draping his arm along the booth behind Hope's shoulders.

"I really *can't*. You see, Dr. Preston is expecting *me* to show you around. It would look bad if Dr. Valencia does my job." He looked pointedly at the other man, who nodded in understanding.

She pursed her lips. "It also looks bad when you show up a half an hour late."

Evan gave her his best panty-melting grin. "True. But my boss doesn't know about that. Be a peach and keep it that way."

"Asshole," she murmured under her breath.

He snatched a fry from her plate and popped it in his mouth with a satisfied smirk.

Francisco slid out of the booth and picked up his tray. "Well, if you don't need me to show you around, I should get back to work."

She smiled brightly at him. "Thank you for saving me."

"Of course. Anytime."

"Maybe we could do it again, soon."

The man coughed as if uncomfortable and glanced away. "I'm sure we'll run into each other again."

Her smile faltered at his noncommittal reply. "Thanks again for lunch."

Francisco waved his hand, and with a sad, puppy dog look, walked away.

That's right, Romeo. Move along.

Hope turned, angling her leg so there was more space between them. Her eyes were back to angry.

"You've got a lot of nerve."

"So I've been told."

"I don't want nor need you to show me around."

"Unfortunately, socialite, you're stuck with me as your tour guide."

"I'll just go to Parker and ask for a new tour guide."

"Aw, you're going to make waves on your second day? He's going to be so disappointed. Here you have him thinking you're such a team player."

Evan had to admit, she had been a team player. That had only made her that much more appealing, which pissed him off.

"I'll simply explain that I fucking hate you."

That would definitely put Evan on Parker's shit list; a place no one wanted to be. Still, he acted unaffected.

"But then I'll have to explain that you let me fuck you in your office on your first day. That might tarnish your *darling* status, sweetheart."

"Don't call me sweetheart, asshole."

"Would you prefer sugar tits?"

"You ever call me that again," she snarled, "and I'll junk punch you."

Somehow, he knew she wasn't bluffing.

"Then don't call me asshole."

She shrugged. "If the shoe fits…"

He blatantly stared at her tits. They looked amazing in the tight bodice of her dress. "Exactly."

"God, I can't stand you."

"And yet, you still want me to fuck you."

She glared up at him, but he noticed she didn't deny it. The feeling was mutual. Getting Steven's little sister to fall in love with him might be a lost cause, but he could get her addicted to his cock.

The problem was, could he not get hooked on her pussy in the process?

"You are such an arrogant son of a bitch." Her nipples poking through her dress suggested his arrogance wasn't a deal breaker. Then her eyes narrowed, and she created more space between them as she looked down at the table. "I'm sure you're already worn out from your morning supply room run."

But him already fucking someone else might be a deal breaker.

He chewed the inside of his mouth and stared at her for a beat before blurting out, "I wasn't in the supply closet, okay? I was dictating reports from last night and lost track of time."

She stared at him, open-mouthed. "Why would you try to make me think that you..."

"Because I'm an asshole, Hope." He snapped his finger by her head. "Keep up."

"So instead of just admitting that..."

"I didn't like how friendly you were being with Francisco."

A slow smirk spread across her face. "Evan Lacroix—were you jealous? Do you looooove me?" And because his twin had made him sit through enough chick flicks to last a lifetime, he knew Hope was channeling Sandra Bullock when she began singsonging, "You think I'm gorgeous... You want to kiss me... You want to hug me..."

He leaned closer and growled in her ear, "I want to fuck you. Right. Now."

Pulling back, she stared into his eyes and swallowed hard before whispering, "I need your word that no one would know. *No one.* Ever."

"I don't kiss and tell, socialite."

But fucking and telling might be a whole other story, when the time was right.

Chapter Nine

Hope
Why did his arrogance have to be like catnip for her? He was right. She still wanted him to fuck her. Ugh. She needed to find a therapist here, STAT.

She fought to maintain a leisurely pace back to her office. Even though she'd walked with male colleagues lots of times, she felt like everyone who walked by them knew what they were on their way to do.

"You should never play poker," Evan remarked with a smirk as they walked the long hallway leading to her office, which was thankfully empty. "Or try to lie in court. You look like you've just committed a crime."

"Well, not a crime, per se. But probably something that's frowned upon."

"Trust me, socialite. No one would begrudge you having your sweet pussy pounded."

"It's not professional."

Her mother would be appalled. One more reason no one could ever know.

"Are you saying you've never messed around at work before?"

She looked up at him as her office door came into view.

"Other than the other day with you? No. Never. I won't even bothering asking the same of you."

"Well, when you work as much as I do, sometimes you have to improvise to get your needs met."

Was that what this was? An improvisation?

Hope didn't want to overanalyze it, but yeah, that's exactly what it was.

She unlocked her office door and stepped inside, letting Evan follow behind. The lamp she'd bought to use instead of the harsh fluorescent overhead one was still on from when she'd dropped her things off this morning. She heard the click of the lock and took a deep breath before turning around to look at the gorgeous man standing by the door.

He'd looked exceptionally sexy when he'd approached her table in his dress shirt and tie. His eyes seemed a deeper shade of blue, and his longer hair was slightly messy, as if he'd run his fingers through it absentmindedly. She'd seen him doing that the other night when he was looking at a patient's chart. It had been endearing at the time—even though she'd thought he was a jerk.

She still thought that, but there was no denying she wanted a repeat of the other day. Maybe this time would only be mediocre, and this would be the last time.

He stalked toward her, his eyes never leaving hers until he was inches from her. Tracing his index finger along her jawline and down her neck, he murmured with a menacing smile, "I believe I said you were going to have to beg this time. On your knees." Then he squeezed her throat softly while he guided her to her knees.

Her panties were already damp as she looked up at him from her submissive position.

Evan unbuckled his belt and opened his trousers to pull his cock out from his boxer briefs. "Beg to suck it," he demanded as he traced her lips with the tip, then rubbed the length along her cheeks.

It was velvety soft and warm. His musk scent made her stomach dip, and she suddenly wanted nothing more than to have him in her mouth.

"Please let me suck your cock."

"Sir," he corrected as he slapped her cheek with his dick.

"Please let me suck your cock, Sir."

He looked down at her with pursed lips, as if he wasn't convinced, so she laid it on thick while cupping his balls and making her eyes wide as she stared back at him.

"Please, Sir. I need to taste you. I'll suck it so good. I want to feel you in my throat." She swirled her tongue along the seam of his balls then murmured, "I'm begging."

He cupped her face, then with the tip of his thumb, tugged her bottom lip down.

"Be sure you do a good job, socialite."

Taking his shaft in her hand, she ran her tongue under his helmet, then licked down his length and back up.

He ran his fingers through her hair and pulled it away from her face, as if he wanted a better view of what she was doing. "That's it. Good girl."

Hope traced along the tip again, then without preamble, engulfed his entire cock, feeling the head bob in her throat.

"Oh fuck!"

She held him in her throat for a few beats before slurping off. With the shaft nice and slippery, she jerked his cock hard before taking him deep again, then began working her mouth and hand in unison.

"Holy fuck." The word lasted a few beats before he grabbed a handful of hair and tugged until she pulled her mouth off. "You need to slow down, socialite."

"Aw, I want to taste you."

"Next time. Right now, I want to bend you over your desk and fuck you hard."

She could work with that.

****

Evan

He reached for her hand to help her up, then holding her by the nape of the neck because she seemed to like that, he guided her to her desk and pushed on her shoulder until she was bent over the top.

With her ass jutting out, he flipped the hem of her skirt onto her back, slid her panties to the side—feeling how wet she was in the process—and thrust his cock as deep in as he could go.

"I love how fucking tight you are," he said through gritted teeth as he pumped in and out of her.

The view of her ass with her panties still on was hot, but he wanted to see her bare ass, so he pulled out long enough to yank the fabric to her knees.

Now *that* was hot as fuck.

Reaching in front, he worked through her folds until he found her clit. He pressed his cock in deep and held it there as he polished her engorged pearl with one hand and covered her mouth with the other when she began to moan loudly.

Her pussy gushed when he did that.

Me likey. His little socialite was a kinky girl. They were going to have a lot of fun together.

She breathed deeply through her nose; her moans muffled until her little body spasmed and her pussy began to milk his cock.

He removed his hand from her mouth and clit and held her hips tight as he fucked her hard and fast, biting back grunts as his balls tightened and he erupted.

He made small, deep thrusts until he'd emptied himself completely inside her. His cum was going to be leaking out of her for days, he thought with a satisfied smile as he slowly pulled out.

"Clean it," he growled, not caring that she was still lying with her face on her desk, panting.

She sat up, bent over at the waist, and licked his cock like a popsicle.

"Such a good slut."

Hope looked at him and smiled as she continued her task.

He leaned over her back and pulled her pussy lips apart with his thumb and index finger to admire his cum dripping from her pussy.

"You are such a dirty girl. I fucking love it."

She stood up straight with a smile.

"I am a dirty girl. And no one will ever know, you got it?"

"Just me."

He liked the idea of being the only one to know this side of her way more than he should.

She swiped between her legs with tissues from the box on her desk as he tucked himself back in his pants.

"We need to talk about this no condom thing."

What about it? He'd loved going bareback with her.

"I thought you were on birth control?"

"I am. But, if you're running off to the supply closet on a regular basis with other people, I think we need to use one."

He opened his mouth to remind her that he hadn't really done that when she continued, "Not that we're exclusive or anything. You can go to the supply closet with whoever you want, and I can bring anyone back to my office that I feel like. But, if we're going to do that, then we need to make sure dicks are wrapped up."

"How about if we don't do that? With other people, I mean."

She pulled her head back and looked at him with furrowed brows, as if confused. "But I don't want to date you."

Ouch.

His face must have conveyed he was slighted because she added, as if to soften the blow, "Not in public, anyway. My brother would lose his shit if I were dating you. Besides, I don't want to mess with your reputation and have women think you're going to take them on a date in the future."

He shrugged. "That's true. I don't date, and I'm normally not exclusive." *And your brother can fuck off.*

"We're not exclusive. Just when it comes to sex. And if there comes a time when we no longer want to be exclusive with that, let's just be honest about it."

"Deal."

She glanced at the Fitbit on her wrist. "Do you have time to show me at least a few departments today?"

He should be thrilled she wanted to fuck and run, but part of him wished she were needy and wanted to cuddle.

"Yeah, I can show you the second floor."

Pulling a compact from her purse, she checked her appearance in the mirror, swiped a finger under her eyes to remove the smudges from her mascara, then applied a fresh coat of lipstick. A minute later, she closed the case with a snap and smiled at him as she slid it back in her purse.

"You'd never know you were just bent over a desk," he said with a smirk as he walked toward the door.

"Unless you examined my panties."

"Which I will happily do, anytime."

Evan pulled open the door to find Parker standing on the other side, his hand poised as if he were about to knock.

"Dr. Preston!" Hope exclaimed. "Did you need me?"

Their boss glanced at Evan, then at Hope. "I was just stopping to see how your tour went."

She glanced nervously at Evan. "We were just about to get started."

"You're just getting started? Don't you have an ER shift soon, Dr. Lacroix?"

"I do. We were going to see the second floor and continue tomorrow. I'm afraid I was dictating reports from last night and lost track of time."

"Then I had to take a phone call," Hope offered. "So, it's just as much my fault that we're so late."

Parker looked at them skeptically, then glowered at Evan. "So I can expect your reports on my desk by tomorrow."

"Absolutely," Evan replied with confidence. Fortunately, he was almost finished. He'd only need to stay an hour late tonight to finish.

"Good, I'll be sure to look for them." There was a warning in his tone and Evan knew he better deliver.

Parker's face softened when he looked back at Hope and pointed over her shoulder into her office. "I see you're almost settled in."

She turned to follow his gaze around her office. Except Evan knew she was looking for evidence they may have left behind.

Turning back with a smile, she replied, "Getting there. I'm planning on spending the rest of the day in the lab, so it won't be today."

"Or tomorrow, apparently." Parker looked over at Evan with a scowl.

Hey, she said she was at fault, too!

Evan knew that didn't matter. Hope was the new darling of Boston General and could do no wrong in their boss's eyes.

"Research shows people tend to remember the first and last things in a session, so it's better to have more mini sessions than one long one," Hope offered. "So this will probably work out better."

It was cute, yet sexy, the way she was trying to defend him.

"As long as you don't mind."

"Not at all. Like I said, this will be better when it comes to trying to remember names and locations—both things I'm notoriously bad at."

"Well, I'll let you get started then. Be sure to let me know if there are any problems or anything you need."

She closed her door and locked it.

"I will. Thanks for coming by to see me."

Parker went his separate way, and Evan had to fight to keep his hand from the small of her back as they walked toward the elevator.

"That was too close for comfort," she murmured.

"Your door was locked. We could have just pretended we weren't there. Well, if you hadn't been making so much damn noise."

"It was hot how you handled it, though."

Evan loved how she owned her kink.

"You dirty girl. I will cover your mouth anytime you want."

She glanced up with a grin. "I hope so."

Chapter Ten

Hope

She woke up the next morning to a text from an unknown number, although she easily figured out it was from Evan based on the context.

Unknown: I'm going to have to postpone our tour until tomorrow. Things are crazy in the ER. I was called in the same time as Steven.

Hope had no idea what time her brother went to work since he—and his dog—had been spending all their time at his girlfriend's. She hadn't seen Lola since last week.

Hope: No problem! I'll see you tomorrow.

It was too early to call Yvette on her commute to the hospital, since it was only six on the West Coast, and her friend kept hours similar to hers. Hope needed to be sure to call her at noon though; there was a lot she needed to catch her friend up on, plus she needed to confirm she was still coming over for the Fourth.

Steve had invited them to his beach house, but after that, they were hitting the bed-and-breakfasts her realtor had emailed her about. Hope was determined to bring her friend closer than three thousand miles away.

She walked in her office and fired her computer up to check her hospital emails. Fortunately, being new, there weren't many. No voicemails either. She kinda liked being the new girl.

Since she wasn't going on a tour today, she would be able to spend more time in the lab. She liked the people working there. They were so meticulous; it was evident how much they cared about their patients. She couldn't wait for her technology from Armstrong Labs to arrive.

But before getting immersed in the lab, she was going to run by the ER to try to see her brother and have a chat about his absence and no communication. If she happened to run into Evan, well, that would just be a coincidence. Nothing more.

Her blond sibling was the first person she spotted when she walked through the double doors.

"Hey, little sister. What brings you down here?"

"Well, you."

Steve lifted his eyebrows. "Me?"

"Yeah, you know, you're supposed to be my roommate and share your sweet dog with me. Since I left Ava and her adorable kids, Lola was going to be my consolation. Except, I've got to spend time with her, what? Maybe two days? Which is more than I've seen my brother. Who, again, is supposed to be my roommate."

He gave her a sheepish grin. "Aw, I'm sorry. I thought you'd like having the place to yourself."

"I mean, I don't mind it. But it has gotten a little lonely. And I don't know the good takeout spots yet."

"The takeout menus are in the drawer by the dishwasher. You can't go wrong with any of those," he said, wrapping his arm around her waist and steering her toward his office. "But I am sorry I haven't been around as much as I should be."

Her brother was in love, for the first time that Hope ever knew about. She couldn't begrudge him spending time with his new girlfriend—although she would like to meet the woman.

They reached his tiny office, and she sat down in the grey fabric chair across the desk from his office chair that was identical to hers. The one she was buying a replacement for.

"It's okay. I'm just being melodramatic. Evan texted me this morning to tell me he came in at the same time as my brother, and I realized I had no idea that time that was and that I hadn't seen you in days."

He narrowed his eyes at her as he took his seat. "Evan Lacroix?"

She nodded her head.

"Why would Evan be texting you?"

"To postpone our tour today. We've only covered the second floor so far, so we're not making much progress."

"Is he being an asshole?"

"Nothing I can't handle."

"It still pisses me off that Parker chose *him* of all people, to be your mentor. If you need me to—"

She interrupted him. "I don't need my big brother to fight my battles. I'm a big girl."

"You're the fucking queen, remember? Make sure you're being treated as such. Boston General is lucky you chose to come here."

"Aw, thanks, Steve."

"I'm serious."

"Well, I'm really liking it here so far. Almost everyone I've met has been so helpful and friendly."

"Except Evan."

"It's fine. Focus on the big picture. I'm happy I chose Boston General."

"I'm glad. I wouldn't have encouraged you to come here if I didn't think you'd be a great fit."

She knew he always had her best interests at heart.

"Let's plan on having dinner tonight. I'll introduce you to Whitney."

"Wow, are you sure?"

The corner of his mouth lifted. "No. But I know it's in my best interest to have you meet her sooner rather than later."

"You really like this woman."

"Yeah, I really do."

"Do you loooove her?" Hope already knew by the way he'd been acting that he did. She just doubted he would admit it.

"I think I do."

His admission caught her off guard. "Damn. I never thought you'd say it out loud. That makes me happy. I can't wait to meet her."

"You better behave yourself. And feel free to eat and run."

"Rude."

He shrugged, unapologetic.

"Don't worry, I'll find something to do after dinner. But I'm not staying out all night."

"I wouldn't expect you to."

"Okay." She stood and walked toward the door. "I have work to do. I'll see you tonight."

She rounded the doorjamb to see Evan walking her way.

Hope got as much distance from Steven's office as she could before meeting him in the hallway.

"If it isn't the darling of Boston General. What are you doing down in the ER?" He gave her a knowing smirk. "Were you hoping to run into me?"

"Pfft, you wish."

He looked her up and down, his eyes resting on the bit of cleavage her blouse was showing. "Yeah, I do."

Hope reached up and tapped under his chin. "Eyes up here, sport."

"Sport? Is that an improvement from 'asshole'?"

"It's probably just a politer version that can be used in public."

"Ah, always the debutante." With a smirk, he leaned closer to murmur in her ear, "Well, not always. For the record, I prefer the slutty side to the socialite."

"Speaking of. My brother has asked me to make myself scarce tonight after dinner—probably around eight. Any ideas what I could do?"

He looked at her with a wicked grin. "I could think of a few."

"I thought so. Text me your address later."

"Do you want to grab a drink or maybe go listen to some music?"

She cocked her head. "Do you not have alcohol at your place? Or a radio?"

"I just thought..."

Hope glanced around to make sure no one could overhear her, then said quietly, "We already talked about this. I don't want to date you—I don't even like you. I just want to have kinky sex with you."

His mouth opened, as if her revelation surprised him, then he flashed her a look of condescension. "You'd be way too high maintenance anyway. The only thing I'm interested in is using your holes until I'm tired of you."

Out of all that, the thing that offended her was being called high maintenance.

"I'm not high maintenance."

Evan scoffed. "Sure you're not."

"I'm not, and I'm offended at the accusation."

He put his hands over his heart with a look of concern on his face. "Oh, no, not offended. How will I ever get to sleep tonight?" Then his face hardened as he removed his hands from his chest and stood up taller while he quickly looked around. "Oh, yeah. Like a log after shooting my cum all over your tits."

The image of him doing just that flashed in her mind and she felt her panties get damp.

"God, you're a jerk."

"So you keep saying, and yet..." He raised his eyebrows with a smirk before walking toward his office. He called over his shoulder, "See you tonight, princess. Try not to think about me too much today."

She'd try, but she didn't know if that was possible.

CHAPTER ELEVEN

Hope

"I can't believe you did the deed with Dr. Dick," her best friend's voice shrieked through her cell phone. Thankfully, she'd gone on a walk during her lunch break and made the call then.

Hope didn't know if Yvette was proud or ashamed of her. Although, given what the two girls knew about each other, she'd assume the former.

"Twice. Hoping for a third time tonight."

"So, I'm guessing you were wrong about him being a dick."

"Oh, no. He's an arrogant prick. Totally not boyfriend material. But he's kinky and dominant."

"He hit the trifecta of your kryptonite. Smart, arrogant asshole, and great in bed."

"I never said he was great in bed."

"You wouldn't have gone back for seconds, let alone thirds, if he wasn't."

"True. And I never said he was smart."

"He's a doctor; I thought it was safe to assume."

"Fair enough. But it's just sex, so he could be stupid for all I care."

"I don't think that's true. You're as sapiosexual as you are submissive. If he were dumb, you wouldn't be interested."

"You think you know me so well," she snarked.

Hope could practically see her friend fold her arms across her chest when Yvette replied, "Am I wrong?"

"No," she bit out. "But he is a jerk, so there's no way I'm getting involved with him. I learned my lesson. Plus, my brother hates him, not to mention we work together, so all of this has to be on the down low."

"Which probably makes it more exciting."

That was true.

"A little."

"Well, as long as you're being careful and don't get attached, I'm happy you're having sex. That makes one of us."

"I already told you—you're going to find Mr. Wonderful when you come visit, fall in love, and move here and go into a bed-and-breakfast partnership with me."

"And for the hundredth time, I already told you: friends and money don't mix."

"They do when there are clear expectations and a contract."

Yvette was silent, so Hope continued, "Just promise you'll be open if something great comes along."

There was a deep sigh on the other end of the line. "You're lucky I love you as much as I do, because I know you're going to be relentless with this."

Hope couldn't help but grin. "I guess you do know me well."

"I do indeed. I have to get to work. I'll talk to you soon."

"Can't wait to see you! Love you!"

"Love you, too."

How could she not want her friend close by? No one knew her quite like Yvette. They'd been friends since middle school and roomed together in college. Yvette was the one person Hope knew she could trust with anything. And vice versa. Hope knew her BFF's skeletons, too, and would take them to the grave.

Chapter Twelve

Evan

He arrived at his brownstone after working twelve hours. He'd been slated to stay until six, but given his evening plans, begged off, citing he needed to sleep before he could work anymore with patients.

It wasn't exactly a lie. He was going home to get some shuteye. But it was so he'd have enough energy to fuck Hope when she showed up later tonight.

Evan walked through the front door and did a quick survey of his place. Fortunately, he had a housekeeper come every other week—not to mention he was rarely home, so it was respectable for company. Even his socialite.

Wait, she's not mine.

He amended his thought. *Respectable for company. Even a socialite.*

After sending her his address, he set his alarm and hoped like hell he'd be able to sleep even though he was keenly anticipating what tonight was going to be like.

Fortunately, he was fucking exhausted. The last thought he had before falling asleep was, "I wonder if anal is a hard limit for her?"

Not surprisingly, he dreamed of butt plugs and dildos and watching Hope put on a show for him, using both.

He woke with an idea.

Hope

In the middle of dinner, she received a text.

Evan: Send me a picture of your tits.

She glanced up to make sure her brother was completely occupied with Whitney before answering.

Hope: Are you crazy? No way.

Evan: Do it. Now.

Hope: I'm not sending you a picture of my boobs so you can blackmail me later with it.

Evan: I'll delete it once you get here. You have my word.

Hope: After you've made a copy.

Evan: You have spectacular tits. Definitely laptop wallpaper worthy, I'm not going to lie. But if I tell you I'll delete it without making a copy, I'll delete it without making a copy. Now send me a picture of your fucking tits.

Hope looked across the table at Steven and Whitney. "Be right back."

"Where are you going?" her brother called after her.

"The bathroom."

She walked through her bedroom to the bathroom and closed and locked the door.

What am I doing? she thought as she lifted her shirt off her head, then undid her bra and dropped it on the floor.

But as she positioned her phone on the counter and cupped her breasts, she had to admit as the camera flashed, she was turned on.

After a couple of tries to get the right angle, she took one she deemed worthy and included it in a text to Evan, with a message, **You owe me**.

She hadn't even finished getting dressed when she heard the ding of a reply.

Evan: Fuck, those are nice!

Followed by, **You'll get what's coming to you, socialite. Don't worry.**

Why did that feel ominous? And exciting?

And still a third text read: **Send me a picture of your fingers in your pussy.**

Hope: No.

Evan: Do it. Now. Or I'm going to spank your ass when you get here and take one myself. Then I'll take another one with my cum dripping out of it.

Oh my god. She didn't know which she wanted more. His threat earlier of coming on her tits or what he'd just described.

Hope: I thought you were coming on my tits tonight.

Evan: Plan on being here a while, socialite. I've got big plans for you.

Hope: I'm not spending the night.

Evan: You weren't invited.

See you soon. Don't be late.

Send me a picture of your fingers in your pussy. NOW.

Hope decided he'd have to be happy with just a picture of her pussy, sans fingers.

Chapter Thirteen

Hope

Evan opened the front door of his brownstone with a genuine smile. "You made it!"

"I did," she said, returning his smile as she walked through the threshold.

He was barefoot, dressed in a pair of faded Levis, a navy-blue T-shirt, and his hair was damp. It had a nice clean smell.

"Your home is beautiful," she said as she surveyed the high ceilings and what appeared to be original crown molding.

"I like it."

He was behind her now, with his hands on her tits, as they continued exchanging pleasantries.

"I need to figure out which area of town I want to move to when Steve kicks me out."

His hand was on her throat. "Brookline, where you're currently at, is nice, but I prefer The Seaport District. I haven't had any problems here. Take off your pants."

When she didn't immediately move her hands to her pants to comply with his demand, he gently squeezed her neck and pushed her against the nearest wall.

"I think you need a lesson in following orders."

Hope let out a little whimper. "Yes, I do."

****

Evan

His sassy submissive. He'd heard the term before, but had never met a woman who it fit, until now. Hope was the walking definition, and it made his dick so hard, he was afraid there were going to be zipper imprints on it.

He tugged her yoga pants down to her ankles, and she obediently kicked them to the side. She wasn't wearing any underwear.

Evan explored her folds with one hand, finding her completely drenched. With his other hand, he pinched her nipple.

"Take your top off."

This time, she immediately grabbed the hem of her T-shirt and lifted it over her head.

"Bra, too."

Again, she moved to comply with his command, and soon her bra was part of the pile of her clothes on the floor by his front door.

She hadn't moved from where he'd placed her against the wall, and he slowly pulled his fingers from her wet pussy. Taking a step back, he scanned her naked body from head to toe.

"Fuck, you're beautiful," he begrudgingly whispered. He couldn't help it—she was perfect. Evan didn't want her to be perfect. He wanted her to be disposable. Forgettable.

So far, Hope Ericson was proving to be neither.

Gently twisting her nipple, he didn't let go as he led her to the couch in the living room. She had to scramble on her tiptoes to keep him from tugging too hard.

He released the pink bud, then leaned down to softly run his tongue around it. She let out another little moan.

Evan sat on the couch, leaving her standing stark naked in front of him. He liked her like this—vulnerable, compliant, and wanting to be fucked.

He reached between her legs and found her so wet, her nectar was running down her inner thighs.

Circling her clit, he growled, "Do you like being my slut, socialite?"

"Yes." She said it so softly, he almost didn't hear her.

He swatted her clit hard. "Sir."

"Yes, Sir." Her whisper was louder this time.

Evan dipped his fingers inside her pussy and finger fucked her slowly.

"Your pussy is so wet. You like being under my control, don't you?"

"I love it."

With his free hand, he spanked her clit again.

"Sir."

She took in a quick breath. Her nipples were hard points.

"I love it, Sir."

"Then why didn't you send me a picture of your fingers in your pussy, like I told you?"

He added a second finger and pressed in deep.

"I-I don't know."

He slapped her clit again and she moaned. That's when he realized she was forgetting the "sir" on purpose for the punishment.

"Sir."

"I don't know, Sir. I did send you one of my pussy."

He added a third finger. "That's not what I asked for, is it?"

"No." Evan delivered rapid swats to her clit until she cried out, "No, Sir!"

"What did I say I was going to do to you if you didn't send me a picture?"

"Spank my ass and take a picture yourself."

Her pussy smelled so good; he couldn't help himself. He leaned forward and circled her clit with his tongue, then pulled it between his lips before releasing it with a *pop*!

"Then what?"

"Then you were going to take another one with your cum dripping from me."

"You liked that idea, didn't you?"

"Yes, Sir." Her whisper was once again soft, as if she were ashamed to admit it.

He moved his thumb around her clit. "Just like you loved the idea of me coming your tits."

She drew in another deep breath and adjusted her feet, as if to maintain her balance. "Yes, Sir."

She was nearing the edge—where he planned on keeping her for most of the night.

Removing his fingers from her pussy, Evan leaned back against the couch cushions and patted his lap.

"Well then, socialite, let's get on with it."

****

Hope

She liked how the fabric of his jeans felt against her bare skin as she lay across his lap. The contrast of Evan being fully clothed while she was naked only added to the element of him being in complete control.

Hope fucking loved it.

He pulled her legs apart and ran his fingers along her seam, then dipped them inside her. She lifted her hips slightly to give him better access and was met with a stinging smack to her butt cheek.

"Put your ass down! And don't you dare come without my permission."

She relaxed back onto his thighs and felt a battery of blows to her ass. All while he maintained finger fucking her.

"Dirty. Fucking. Girl," he snarled as he delivered a hard slap with each word. "When I tell you to do something, you fucking do it."

Her mind immediately went to *dream on, buddy*. But then she decided when it came to sex, she could comply. Happily.

"Yes, Sir."

He removed all but his middle finger from her pussy and she saw the flash of the camera. Evan set his phone in front of her face. An image of his finger in her pussy, her ass flaming red, was on the screen.

It was debasing. And it was hot.

"God, you're such a slut." He moaned as he pushed a second digit inside her. "Your pussy just gushed when you looked at that."

It wasn't like she could deny it, so she might as well embrace it. She'd make sure he deleted the pictures—later.

He moved his hand to rub her clit fast, and she moaned out loud. More hard slaps rained down on her ass, then her head jerked back slightly when he tugged on her hair.

"Get up."

Hope scurried off his lap, and he pulled her by her tresses to the end of the couch, then pressed her upper body down so her ass was on full display and her face and chest were in the cushions.

She heard the rustle of him undressing, then felt his hand on her hip while he lined up his cock to her entrance. With one swift thrust, he was in her balls deep. His fingers gripped her hipbones tight, and he roared loudly, "Fuck!"

Hope liked the idea of him losing control because of her. Yeah, she was playing the role of submissive, but she knew there was power with that.

"Your pussy feels so damn good." He grunted as he began to move in and out of her.

"So does your cock."

He gave her a quick tap to the butt. "Sir."

She arched her back and purred, "So does your cock, Sir."

"Dirty girl. Remember what I said about coming."

Oh, she remembered. He'd pushed her to the brink, only to back off before she could go over the ledge—with or without permission, more than once.

"What if I come without permission, Sir?"

"I'm going to fuck your ass with my cock while I make you ride a dildo."

"Oh god," she panted as his words caused the orgasm to erupt from her toes. Her body convulsed like she was possessed. When she'd stilled, he drove into her with fury, grunting loudly until he held her hips tightly as he emptied himself inside with a roar.

While she struggled to find her breath, Evan laid his bare chest across her back and murmured softly in her ear, "I love how naughty you are. And you're going to be punished for coming without permission."

That's what she was hoping for.

He pulled out and a few seconds later, she felt his hand spread her pussy apart and another flash went off.

She heard him chuckling and stood up to find him admiring the photo on his screen. He flashed it toward her with a smirk. "That's the money shot, right there."

She glanced at the image. It was pretty hot.

"Which you're going to delete before I leave tonight."

"Aw, come on." He went back to studying it. "Let me have this one. You can't see your face."

"No."

"How about I let you take one of my dick? Then we're even."

"Oh, please. Guys send out dick pics like they're greeting cards. Like you'd care if a picture of your cock got circulated."

He glanced down at his appendage still jutting out proudly. "It *is* pretty impressive, huh?"

She smiled in spite of herself.

Using his T-shirt, he swiped between her legs, then pulled a blanket out of a basket by the couch and wrapped it around her shoulders.

"Are you thirsty? Hungry?" He kissed her temple. "You need to hydrate before I have my way with you again."

Chapter Fourteen

Hope

She jerked awake with a gasp when the ringtone she had for Steven started going off. Evan's arm was heavy, draped around her bare middle, and she lifted it off her to roll over and search for her phone.

She groaned out loud when she saw the time on his bedside clock. It was almost three. Way past closing time for the bars. Where was she going to say she'd been?

Fuck.

Hope found her purse and hurriedly pulled her phone out before it stopped ringing.

"I'm so sorry!" she whispered. "We all fell asleep watching a movie."

"Where are you?"

She tried to evade the question. "I'm leaving in five minutes. I should be home in fifteen minutes. I'm so sorry. I hope I didn't worry you."

"Well, yeah, you kind of did. I didn't know if you'd gotten lost, or worse."

She wanted to point out that she had GPS on her phone, but decided now wasn't the time to be sassy. Contrite would be the better approach.

"I know. I know. I feel terrible. But I'm okay, and I'll be home soon. Please go back to bed."

"Where are you?" he asked again.

Shit, what was that friendly nurse's name?

In her groggy condition, she couldn't recall the woman's name, so she blurted out one of guys from the lab.

"Liam's. A bunch of us from the lab decided to hang out at his place and watch movies. We must be working too much, because we all fell asleep and we'd barely had anything to drink."

Hope noticed Evan was now sitting up in bed and smirking at her. Even with his hair sticking up on end and sleepy eyes, he was still sexy. Damn him.

"Are you okay to drive?" Steven asked, concern in his voice. "Maybe you should just stay there."

She gathered her clothes. "No, I'm okay. I'm glad you woke me up." Hope shot Evan a look. "The couch here isn't that comfortable."

Evan rolled his eyes and subtly shook his head, smirk still intact.

"Drive safely."

"I'll be quiet when I come in."

"Lola might have other plans."

Shit. Of course, Lola will yelp in excitement at her arrival. The pup didn't have to get up in the morning and could sleep all day. What else did she have to do but wake up at the sound of someone coming through the front door?

Hope put the phone in the crook of her neck and slipped one arm through a bra strap, followed by the other.

"God, I feel like such a jerk. I know you need your sleep."

"Hope, don't worry about it. I'm just glad you're okay and are on your way. We'll talk more when you get here."

No, no, no!

She fastened her bra strap and started tugging her leggings on, then stopped when she realized she still had cum between her thighs. She looked over to see Evan's obvious amusement at her dilemma.

"Please go back to bed. I'll feel terrible if you're still up when I get home."

"I'll try. Let's get lunch together tomorrow, though."

"Sounds great. Come find me—" She stopped when she realized she didn't want to run the risk of him talking to someone in the lab and mentioning tonight. Something Steven totally would do. "You know what? I'll come down to the ER around noon. If you're available, we'll go."

"That will work. I'll talk to you soon. Love you."

"Love you, too."

She let out a big sigh once she disconnected the call and looked over at Evan, still in bed.

"How did we fall asleep?"

He swung his legs to the side of the bed and stood. Unabashed at being as naked as the day he was born.

"Well, I don't know if you remember, but we did some pretty tiring things."

"You did do a lot of work," she conceded with a giggle as she remembered all the things they'd done last night.

Evan walked into his bathroom and returned a moment later. He dropped to his knees in front of her and cleaned between her thighs and pussy with a warm washcloth.

She resisted the urge to tidy his hair.

"Careful. I might start to think you've got a nice side."

He stood and tossed the washcloth toward his hamper in the corner.

"I do have a nice side. Ask my patients, or my family. Hell, anyone I work with other than your brother—unless I've slept with them, then they might disagree."

She'd seen him in action with his patients, so she knew at least part of what he was saying was true.

"Then why are you such a jerk with me?"

The corner of his mouth turned up. "Because you like it."

Was that true?

Hope tugged her yoga pants on over her feet. "Maybe. I guess it makes it easier to keep this just about sex."

"And that's all this can be?"

Was she imagining it, or did his tone sound hopeful?

"Well, since you're a serial bachelor, and you and my brother hate each other—it's for the best. Besides, I just started at the hospital—I don't need the reputation of being the new girl who naively tried taming the resident bad boy."

"An impossible feat."

"Exactly."

"So, we'll just keep screwing each other's brains out in private and act like we just met when in public?"

She let out a little chuckle. "Or you could try acting professionally."

He let out a sigh, as if that was going to be a lot of work for him. "I guess."

"Beginning tomorrow, when we continue the tour."

"Fine, but I'm fucking you in your office afterward."

"We'll see. Did you delete those pictures?"

"All but the one."

"Evan! You have to delete *all* of them!"

"Just let me keep it until I fuck you again."

"Tomorrow?"

"Sure."

He didn't sound convincing, and yet she still found herself acquiescing. Maybe because the idea of him wanting to keep it made her feel sexy.

Narrowing her eyes, she sternly pointed her finger at him. "Nobody sees that photo but you. Do you understand?"

"Come on, Hope. I know you think I'm a cad, but I'm not fifteen. I do know how to have some discretion."

He pulled on a pair of pajama pants and walked toward the door with her. She expected him to open the door and send her on her way, but he put his feet in a pair of slippers and walked her to her Tesla.

Opening the driver's door, he waited until she was situated before leaning in and saying, "You could have stayed over, you know."

"No, it's better this way. Keeps everything in perspective."

He shrugged. "I guess." Then he closed the door.

She started the car and rolled down her window.

"Thanks for having me over tonight."

He huffed out a laugh. "I came in your pussy twice and once on your tits. You're welcome anytime." A grin escaped his lips, and he leaned down to murmur, "Slut." Then he stood up straighter and winked. "Drive safely. Send me a text when you get home."

Aw, Dr. Dick is worried about me.

"I will."

She started rolling up her window but stopped when he added, "And don't forget, or I'll call you and then you'll have to explain to your brother why someone is calling at four in the morning."

She gave him an upside-down smile. "I promise. I'll text when I'm home."

"And inside. Not when you've parked but still have to go through the parking lot."

"Are you this protective of all your trysts?"

"No, because it's usually me sneaking out of her place."

"Ew, sneaking?"

He shrugged. "It's easier. Less awkward."

She shook her head. "Coward."

"Maybe. But it saves me from having to have the awkward *morning after* conversation."

"Shouldn't you already have discussed that, prior to the morning?"

"Oh, I do. But women often think sex changes things. Like they have the magic pussy that will make me change my ways."

"I think that would take more than magic."

He stared at her for a beat, then said softly, "It would take someone special, for sure."

"Stop it!"

He furrowed his brows. "Stop what?"

"Looking at me like that. This can never be anything more than sex. We're just two kinky people helping scratch each other's itch. Don't go changing your ways for me."

Evan scoffed. "Don't flatter yourself, socialite."

"See you tomorrow," she bit out.

"Don't forget to text me."

"Yeah, yeah."

"Hope." His tone was stern, like it tended to be when she allowed him to dominate her. "I mean it."

"I already promised I would."

She rolled up her window and gave a wave as she drove off; leaving him standing at the curb in his slippers.

About five minutes later, a text came in. She knew it had to be from Evan; she'd read it when she got home.

Chapter Fifteen

Evan

He was still undecided if he'd be able to get Hope to fall in love with him.

Their sexual compatibility was off the charts; he'd never met someone like her. But with their clothes on, they were constantly at each other's throats. Yet, even that felt like foreplay.

Why'd she have to be so damn smart? And beautiful? And worst of all, an Ericson?

But it was the fact that she was Steven's sister that had made him so determined. He'd avenge Olivia one way or another.

A text came in and he smiled. *Good girl.*

Hope: I'm home in bed.

That's it?

Nothing about the dick pic he'd sent after she left? He'd thought it only fair, since he had no intention of deleting the picture of her pussy leaking his cum.

Evan: Good girl for remembering. I'll be sure to reward you tomorrow.

Hope: I'm glad you didn't consider your dick pic as a reward.

Evan: Come on. You know it's impressive.

Hope: I'll give you that it is, in person. But why would you think I wanted a picture of it?

Evan: I just thought it'd make us even.

Hope: I guess I'll hang on to it as insurance. Although with how proud you seem to be of it, I'd be willing to bet there's already a few in circulation.

Okay, she wasn't wrong. There might be a few photos of his cock floating around in cyberspace.

Evan: But none with your pussy juice still on it.

He'd been trying to be cocky and keep her in her place. Leave it to Hope to blow that all to hell.

Hope: Make sure you shower. Nobody likes a crusty dick.

Evan: It'll be nice and clean for you to sit on tomorrow, socialite. Don't you worry. Be sure to wear a dress tomorrow.

Hope: Good night.

It really had been.

Chapter Sixteen

Hope

She was tempted to wear pants to work, just to make sure Evan knew he wasn't the boss of her. But she had to admit, a dress would make it much easier for a quickie in her office. And she was all for that.

Hope chose a sleeveless solid olive-green A-line dress with a fitted bodice that came right above her knee, along with her favorite nude-colored heels.

Growing up self-conscious of her five-foot eight-inch height, it'd only been in the last few years that she'd embraced wearing heels. Now they were the only thing she wore to work, unless she was there in yoga pants on the weekend.

She took the time to make sure her makeup was on-point and her hair was styled and not just put up in a ponytail—although that would inevitably happen once she entered the lab this afternoon.

Pressing her lips together to make sure her lipstick was even, Hope dropped her wallet and hospital ID in the Chanel bag that matched her shoes. She made sure to give Lola one more treat before she grabbed her keys from the bowl on the table by the door and headed out.

She bounced through the hospital door, ready to take on the day and look good doing it.

"Hello, Henry." She beamed at the security guard who reminded her of Barney Fife from the *Mayberry R.F.D.* show she used to watch on the TV Land channel as a kid.

The older man tipped his pretend hat. "Morning, Dr. Ericson!"

"It's just Hope, Henry. I've told you, Dr. Ericson is my brother."

That elicited a chuckle from him, but she knew he'd call her *doctor* again tomorrow, no matter how many times she'd told him she wasn't one.

"Good morning, Eleanor!" she called brightly to the volunteer working the help desk. "Love your blouse!"

"You look as beautiful as ever, Hope."

That made her smile as she made her way to the elevator. Hope *felt* beautiful this morning. Life was good—she had a job doing something she loved, and she made a damn nice living in the process. Her family was all healthy and she could always count on them to be there for her. She had good friends—granted, they were back in California, but she knew she'd meet new people here, too. And she was having mind blowing sex regularly. What the hell could she complain about?

Famous last words.

Her phone rang as soon as she turned on the light to her office.

"Hi, Mom," she said, opening her bottom desk drawer and dropping her purse inside. She glanced at the Fitbit on her wrist that read nine thirty, which meant it was six thirty in California. "Everything okay? You're calling early."

"I thought I'd try to catch you on your way to work. It seems that's the only time you take my call anymore."

"Well, I just walked into my office and I answered your call, so I just disproved that. How are you? How's Dad?"

"Your father is fine. Working as much as ever, even though he was supposed to slow down and hear fewer cases in lieu of retiring outright."

Hope knew the only way her father would slow down would be if he stopped working altogether. Otherwise, he didn't know how. He'd been a federal judge for as long as she could remember.

"Well, he probably doesn't want to sit home bored while you're off working on all your charities."

"I told him that his help would be welcomed."

"Dad's always been more of a silent supporter, Mom. You know that."

A dramatic sigh came through her phone. "I do."

There was a pause, so Hope asked again, "What's up? Everything else okay?"

"Your brother says he thinks you're dating someone. You didn't come home last night."

Steven ratted her out? Payback was going to be a bitch.

"When did you even have time to talk to him? And for the record, I came home, it was just late."

"I just got off the phone with him. So, it's true? You're seeing someone?"

"No. Nothing like that. He knows I was out with a group of friends, and we all fell asleep watching a movie. I think he's trying to take the spotlight off himself, since he's the one with the girlfriend. He's only stayed at the condo two nights since I got here—the first night I arrived and last night. And last night, his girlfriend came over. Seems pretty serious."

That should throw her mother off her scent and refocus it on her brother. Served him right.

"He failed to mention that part. Tell me more about her. Did you meet her?"

"I did, and she's great. They're a perfect match. Her name's Whitney Hayes and she's a Harvard Law grad, practicing here in Boston. You should ask him about her."

She almost felt bad about throwing him under the bus, but then remembered, he started it.

"I will definitely do that. Are you still glad you chose to go to Boston?"

She looked around her office that was almost completely unpacked and smiled. "Yeah, I am."

"We'll talk this winter."

"Now I have a reason to buy winter clothes. I've always wanted to have a seasonal wardrobe, but it wasn't very practical in San Diego."

"You had winter clothes here, Hope Francine."

First and middle name. She'd obviously offended her mother—who truly was a socialite. Part of the reason that Evan calling her that didn't bother her, even though she knew he meant it as a slight.

"Yes, of course I did. I just meant that I also had to keep my summer clothes handy because I never knew if it was going to be a shorts or a sweater day. I won't have to worry about that here."

That seemed to appease Francine, who Hope was named after.

"Oh. I see what you mean. Yes, I suppose you won't be wearing shorts there in December."

"But I will be wearing them in San Diego in December when I come home."

There, something else to appease her mom with.

"Oh, that's wonderful news! Your sisters are going to be thrilled. Is Steven coming with you?"

"We haven't talked about it. He's only been home two nights, remember? And he has a girlfriend now. They might make plans with her family, you never know."

"Talk to him, will you? Make sure he knows we'd love to meet Whitney and remind him that the holidays would be a perfect time for that."

"I will. I've got to get to work, Mom. Thanks for calling. I miss you. Give my love to everyone."

"Will do. Love you, too."

She clicked off and immersed herself in paperwork until she heard a knock on her open door and looked up to see Evan standing in the doorway. He looked handsome in black slacks, shiny black shoes, a light grey button-down, and darker grey tie under his white lab coat.

"Good morning, socialite."

She blinked slowly at him. "Wow, is it noon already?"

"No, it's eleven thirty." He stepped inside her office and closed the door, a small smirk escaping his mouth as he stepped closer to where she was sitting behind her desk. "I see you wore a dress. Good girl."

Hope glanced down at her outfit, as if to verify he was right. "I did."

He reached for her hands and pulled her to a standing position, then took a step back, as if to better examine what she was wearing.

"You look beautiful. I like the shoes."

She eyed him suspiciously. "Are you complimenting me? For real?"

Evan let out an uncomfortable chuckle. "Yeah, socialite. I've complimented you before."

"No, you haven't."

"I'm sure I have. Can't you just take the compliment graciously and say thank you like someone who was raised with manners?"

Francine Ericson's ears had to be ringing at that remark.

"You're right. That was rude. I apologize."

He plopped into her chair with a grin. "You can make it up to me by lifting your dress and bouncing on my dick."

Part of her wished her sensibilities were offended at his crudeness and arrogance, but alas, it only served to turn her on.

His cock was already hard when he unbuttoned his pants and slid them down to his ankles. He only took one shoe and pant leg off.

Reaching under her dress, he moved her panties to the side and began rubbing her pussy.

"I love that you're already wet for me."

"I love that you're already hard for me," she sassed back, although she widened her stance as she did.

Evan plunged one finger inside her. "Beautiful, I get hard just thinking about being naked with you."

Hope reached for his shoulder for balance, not trusting her legs not to give out when he smeared her juices onto her clit and began moving his fingers in circles around it.

She let out a whimper, and he removed his hand, tugged her panties to her calves until gravity took over, then spun her around so her back was to him.

Flipping her dress up to her lower back, he put his hand on her hipbones and guided her entrance to his cock, where she sank down while they both let out a soft moan.

She slowly moved up and down, then stopped. "Did you lock the door?"

"Of course."

The chair squeaked when she resumed her rhythm, and she immediately stopped again.

"That's not going to work." He chuckled. Hope moved to get off him, but he held her in place—his cock impaled in her pussy and moved his thighs between hers so she had no choice but to lean back against his chest with her legs spread wide, her ankles wrapped around his calves.

She felt very exposed.

Lifting her dress to her waist, his fingers found her clit again, and he began to rub in firm, leisurely circles.

"Keep your legs spread," he snarled in her ear when her thighs involuntarily clenched.

Evan fondled her left breast with his left hand while his right continued manipulating her sensitive spot. His cock was still inside her pussy, but he wasn't thrusting up.

She let out a low moan, and his left hand moved up to cover her mouth as the pace of his right hand increased. His hand smelled like disinfectant soap.

Hope could still breathe through her nose, but the restriction of her breath through her mouth amplified her arousal.

Then he growled more dirty words in her ear.

"You dirty little whore, sitting here with your cunt on display so I can play with it."

Her breathing picked up, the sound accentuated by his hand over her mouth.

"Shut up and take it."

And the one that pushed her over the edge, "Come all over my cock, bitch."

Her body stiffened, and she arched her back against his chest as she let out a long, muffled moan against his hand.

"That's it, baby." His low and sexy voice was reassuring as her body shuddered with no control.

When she stilled, Hope felt him kiss her hair while he removed his hand from her mouth.

"Fuck, you're sexy."

"I've never felt so uninhibited before," she confessed in a whisper. "You do that to me."

She felt his smile against her hair. "I like being the one to bring that out in you." His tone turned ominous. "Now bend over your desk."

****

Evan

Her face was flushed when they walked out of her office five minutes before noon.

Other than pink cheeks, she looked impeccable—not a hair was out of place and her lipstick had been carefully reapplied. Which only made him want to see it smeared all over his cock.

The plan was to make her fall in love with him, or at least get her hooked on his cock, but he was starting to worry about himself.

He'd been holding her when she fell asleep last night in his bed. And rather than wake her up and send her on her way like he normally would have, he closed his eyes and dozed off—purposefully—with the scent of her floral shampoo filling his senses.

He'd actually been disappointed when she left in the middle of the night. What was up with that?

Even his best friend, Tyler, said, "Uh-oh," with a big 'ol grin when Evan casually mentioned being her mentor doctor when they went to happy hour yesterday.

"What do you mean, 'Uh-oh'? There's no uh-oh."

"Dude, you've never described a woman using words like *smart* or *pioneering*. And the fact that she seems to have gotten under your skin—"

"It's because she's stubborn as fuck," Evan interrupted.

Tyler's smile only grew. "My *uh-oh* stands."

"Fuck off. She's Steven Ericson's sister."

"A challenge. You love challenges."

Evan was itching to tell his best friend that he'd already fucked her multiple times. But keeping things between him and Hope off the radar—for now—was the smart play. And he couldn't tell him about his plan without betraying Olivia's confidence, otherwise he'd just look like an asshole.

Which he was. But he'd rather Tyler not know that about him. Evan wasn't necessarily proud of it.

His buddy knew Evan and Steven disliked each other, but being a radiologist at Boston General, Tyler just chalked it up to two alpha males butting heads. Evan couldn't set the record straight and not out Olivia, so he bit his tongue and let him think that was the reason.

Without the background, Evan's plan would just seem juvenile and vindictive.

And maybe it was. But that fucker Ericson deserved it.

So he kept his mouth shut, even though he was dying to tell his best friend more.

"You've got it all wrong. She's simply a colleague that I've been assigned to help acclimate here. Being with Julia has turned you into a sappy romantic."

Just the mention of his fiancée's name had the radiologist grinning from ear to ear. "If everyone felt about someone the way I do about her, there would be no more wars. Of course, I want that for you, too."

"I'll stick to my philandering ways, thank you."

With a knowing smile, Tyler jerked his chin at him. "We'll see."

Now, he was fighting the urge to put his hand at the small of her back as they walked through the hospital and wanted to punch every fucker that smiled too wide or got too close when Evan introduced her.

They'd just finished the third floor and were standing at the elevators when she said, "Can we do the next floor tomorrow? This is exhausting; I don't think my brain can handle meeting anyone else today."

He was on board. "Sure. Let's have lunch."

Chapter Seventeen

Hope

"I think you just wanted a reason to see me tomorrow," Evan said with a grin as they set their trays down on an outdoor table.

"You're on to me."

The tour had been exhausting, but now that he mentioned she'd see him tomorrow... well, she wasn't mad about it.

"Sweethe—" He stopped. He'd remembered she told him not to call her that. Why did that make her stomach dip? "Baby, all you have to do is ask. I'll come fuck you anytime. No pretense needed."

He took a bite of his salad with a smirk.

"I'm tired and continuing would have been a waste because I'd forget everything," she said with a stern tone. "There was no grand plan to make sure I see you tomorrow."

"Good, because I'm off tomorrow. Not that I wouldn't be willing to come in and take care of your needs, but we'll have to skip the tour until Monday."

The idea shouldn't be as appealing as it was.

"Wow, you need a life. Don't you already have plans on your day off?"

His smile caught her off guard, or maybe it was what he said. "I'd cancel them."

"Don't get all charming on me now. It's weird. I'm already a sure thing, remember?"

He held her gaze for a beat before uttering, "Oh, I remember."

Things were getting too intense for comfort.

She picked up her water and took a sip before asking, "So, what *are* your plans tomorrow?"

"An extra-long workout at the gym, get some laundry done, probably pay some bills…"

"Your life sounds as exciting as mine."

"It's funny, but my life somehow got a lot more exciting almost a week ago."

She raised her eyebrows at him. "What did I say about any attempt to be charming?"

He lifted his shoulders. "I can't help it, I'm naturally delightful." He gave her a wink, then asked, "What about you? What are your plans this weekend?"

"Not much. I have a few boxes I still need to unpack, then I should find a storage unit to move the rest of my stuff into until I get my own place."

"Do you want some help?"

She tilted her head, trying to gauge if he was teasing. His expression remained neutral as he blinked back at her.

"Are you volunteering to help me move boxes into storage?"

"Yeah. Maybe we could get some dinner too. Or breakfast."

Hope's eyes widened at the implication, so he quickly added, "Just depending on the time of day."

"Like a date? I already told you, I can't date you."

"No, not a date. You know how you're supposed to pay people who help you move with pizza? Well, I'm a little more expensive, that's all."

"You don't like pizza?"

"Of course, I like pizza. But I prefer you buy me dinner instead. That's all. Not a date."

"Okay. As long as it's not a date."

"Not a date," he reiterated.

****

Evan

Of course, it was going to be a fucking date, but he found himself liking the idea of not calling it that as much as she did.

He didn't date.

Then again, he didn't fall asleep with a woman either, or fuck her multiple days in a row. Or give her a second thought when he wasn't with her.

But that's exactly what Evan had been doing this week.

Just part of the plan, he reassured himself when he woke up Friday morning and found himself seriously considering going into the hospital—on his fucking day off.

He settled for sending her a text around noon.

Evan: Miss me?

The three dots indicating her reply showed up right away.

Hope: Like I'd miss a rash.

That made him laugh. Her sassiness was his favorite thing about her… well, other than the obvious.

Evan: Are you going to happy hour tonight? Usually people working the day shift on Friday go to Maloney's, the bar down the road, after work.

Hope: I didn't know about it.

Evan: Now you do. It'd be a good chance for you to meet more people.

Hope: Good point. Are you going?

Evan: Am I working?

Hope: I was just asking. Put your claws away, kitty.

Of course he was going. He just needed her to say she was, too. There wasn't a chance in hell he was going to leave her alone with those smooth cardiothoracic assholes. One of them would have her charmed naked before she knew what hit her.

Evan: Aw, do you want me to go?

She sent an emoji of an eye roll.

Hope: Yes, so then I for sure won't go.

Evan: You don't want to go?

Hope: I know this is hard to believe, but going out with a group of people I don't know doesn't sound like my idea of a fun night.

Evan: What does sound like a fun night?

Hope: Honestly? Going home, taking Steve's dog for a walk then changing into my pajamas, ordering takeout, and watching Netflix.

Evan: If you wanted to Netflix and chill, you should have just said so. I'll bring Italian.

He was trying to get a rise out of her, so you could have knocked him over with a feather when she replied, **Bring tacos.**

His heart rate picked up and he couldn't reply fast enough. **What time?**

Hope: Let me check and see if Steve's going to the Cape this weekend. I'll get back to you later.

Evan: I'll be waiting, socialite.

Chapter Eighteen

Evan

He stopped at Taquiera Rosita's Mexican food truck for a dozen *carne asada* street tacos, beans, and rice, then headed to the address Hope had texted him. He'd order dessert from GrubHub and have it delivered to them later.

After punching in the code she'd given him for the gated lot, he backed his Mercedes into an uncovered parking space in the far corner.

Hope greeted him at the door wearing black yoga pants with a big floral pattern of pinks and oranges, and a pink tank top. He didn't know which looked hotter—her ass or her tits. Then her boobs spilled out when she leaned over to put her hand on the collar of the cutest grey mutt he'd ever seen, and he decided, *her tits. Definitely.*

"This is Lola. She'll be hanging out with us tonight."

"Hi Lola." Evan reached his hand down to let the dog smell him. After two sniffs, the pup licked his hand and Hope let go of her collar. Lola nudged his hand with her head in an obvious attempt to get him to pet her.

Evan dropped to one knee and scratched behind the ears; the dog's long, furry tail thumping furiously on the floor the whole time.

"I don't know how, but you've got her approval." Hope took the bag of food from him and turned on the ball of her bare foot and called over her shoulder, "Normally she's a better judge of character."

"Hey, I brought you tacos!"

"That's the only reason I let you in the door."

The view of her walking away had him reconsidering his previous determination. *No, her ass. Definitely her ass.*

He glanced around the entry of the upscale condominium with more square footage than some houses. As Evan followed Hope to the living room, he noticed the place had a sterile feel that sometimes came from having a professional decorator. There was nothing personal on display that indicated who lived there.

"How long has your brother had this place?"

She glanced toward the ceiling, as if she was trying to remember. "Maybe six years? He bought it right after he started at the hospital." She bit the corner of her bottom lip and stared at nothing, like she was deep in thought. "Yeah, it was right when I turned twenty-one. My mother was crying when I came over for my birthday dinner. That was what sealed it for her that he wasn't moving back to California."

"Were you sad, too?"

Maybe the two weren't that close—she just confirmed the eleven-year age gap, since Evan knew Steven was his age.

"Yeah, I was. Then he flew me out to spend a week with him, and I could tell how much he liked it here." She pulled the plates and silverware from the bag and set them on the coffee table, followed by the boxes of food. "How could I be sad when he seemed so content? And now... He obviously was meant to be here."

"Now?"

She paused her task of opening the containers. "If he wasn't here, he never would have met Whitney. I've never seen him this happy."

Bile rose in Evan's throat. That motherfucker didn't deserve happiness.

He gave her a small smile as he opened the boxes of the beans, then the rice in front of him. "Well, if he wouldn't have moved here, then you wouldn't have either, so lucky for me that he did."

"Wow." She glanced at him as she piled tacos on a plate, then handed it to him. "That must have been painful to say out loud, even if you didn't mean it."

"Why would you say that?"

She plopped tacos on another plate. "Seriously? You and my brother can't stand each other, although I have no idea why. Professional rivalry doesn't make sense."

He took her plate and put beans and rice on it for her. "No, why would you say that I didn't mean it"

"So, you're telling me you're happy my brother moved to Boston?"

"No, I'm happy *you* moved to Boston. I recognize that wouldn't have happened if he hadn't, so by extension..."

"If you look me in the face and say you're glad he did, I'll never believe another word you say because I'll know how good of a liar you really are."

"All right, I won't say I'm *glad*. How about appreciative?"

She bit into one of the complimentary chips included with their order. "What's gotten into you?"

"What do you mean?"

"Why are you being... almost... pleasant? It's very confusing. Stop it."

"Stop being pleasant?"

"Yes. The fact that you're an asshole has made it easier to compartmentalize what this is between us. I can't go liking you. That will ruin everything. So, yes, stop it."

"Maybe I'm not normally an asshole—maybe *you* bring it out in me. Have you ever thought of that?"

"No! Why would I? I like how things are. Frankly, I like that you're an asshole—especially in bed. It's hot."

"Sorry, sugar. But if I were truly an asshole, I wouldn't have brought you tacos."

She bit into her taco, closed her eyes, and moaned with her mouth full of food. "So good." Swallowing, she glared at him. "Damn you, and your delicious tacos, Evan Lacroix."

He grinned and pointed the remote at the TV. "What are we watching?"

"You pick, as long as it's not horror." She shifted her right foot under her left thigh and took another bite while he chose a rom-com. She pursed her lips and gave him the side-eye as she muttered, "The first time you're gentle in bed, we're done."

He winked at her. "Don't worry, socialite. I promise to still pull your hair and talk dirty when I'm fucking you."

Hope leaned forward and set her plate on the coffee table, then turned her body so her back was against the armrest and put her feet in his lap.

"I won't hate you if you demonstrate your pleasantry by rubbing my feet, though."

Without a word, he took her foot in his hands and pressed into the arch with his thumbs. She let out a small groan of approval and he tried to hide his smile as he moved up toward her toes. Maybe getting her to fall in love with him wasn't going to be impossible after all.

****

Hope

She flopped onto her back and stared at the ceiling while trying to catch her breath. She needn't had worried. Evan hadn't missed a beat in the dirty, dominant sex department.

The mattress adjusted as he stood and disappeared into her bathroom, then returned a second later with her bath towel that had been hanging on the towel bar.

"Sorry, it was all I could find," he murmured as he swiped between her legs with it. Hope sat up and took over.

"That's fine. I haven't unpacked any linens—Steve has more than enough, but he keeps them in the linen closet in the hall."

Her phone buzzed on the bedside table, and she lunged for it. Steve hadn't said when he was going to be home, and she didn't want to find out he was on his way with Evan still there, naked.

"New boyfriend?" he asked as she peered at the screen.

"No, my brother. He's not going to be home until he picks Lola up in the morning. He and Whitney are taking their dogs to his house on the Cape."

"Good to know."

"That it wasn't a new boyfriend or that my brother won't be back until morning?" she teased.

"Both."

Hope swung her feet onto the ground. "Yeah, but that means I need to let Lola out."

Evan squeezed her shoulder. "Get back in bed. I'll let her out."

"Are you sure you don't mind?" she asked, even as she was burrowing under the still-warm covers while he pulled his jeans on.

"Positive."

"You don't need to leash her up or anything. The little area off the back door in the kitchen is fenced. She's usually pretty quick this time of night."

"Got it."

He looked hot as hell standing there in nothing but a well-worn pair of jeans and just-been-fucked hair.

"Thanks."

With a wink, he replied softly, "No problem, socialite."

Tacos, a foot rub, deliciously dirty sex, and now this? She needed to be careful and not let him lull her into thinking he was a good guy with a dirty mouth. There was no way she could fall for him. Not if she wanted to maintain any kind of relationship with her brother.

She liked him better when she could count on him being an asshole.

The angel—or devil—on her shoulder whispered, "Do ya, though?"

"Yes!" she hissed out loud to nobody but herself. Nice guys involved feelings. Meaningless kinky sex didn't.

Her therapist's voice saying, "You can have both, you know," rang in her ears.

Maybe she could. But it couldn't be with Evan Lacroix.

Chapter Nineteen

Evan

It took a second for him to remember where he was when his eyes fluttered open at the sound of dogs barking. The sun peeking through the blinds told him it was already morning.

He jerked with a start. *Shit!* He was supposed to have left by now. Hope had made him promise he'd be gone before the sun came up and had even set an alarm on her Fitbit.

What happened?

Evan reached for her—the bed still warm where she should be lying.

There was a hand on his shoulder. Hope stood next to the bed with a terrycloth robe tied tight at the waist. Her hair was messy from sleep and sex, and she didn't have a drop of makeup on. She'd never looked more beautiful.

She put a finger to her lips and mouthed *stay here*. He nodded and sat up in bed—causing the frame to creak. Her eyes got big, and she mouthed *be quiet!*

Sorry! He mouthed back.

Hope slipped out the bedroom door, making sure it was closed behind her.

Evan heard female voices coming from what he thought was the kitchen, along with dogs zooming up and down the hall. There was also the sound of water moving through the pipes in the walls. All that combined made it impossible to make out what was being said.

He assumed Steven had come home to shower and get his dog before leaving for Cape Cod for the weekend and had brought his girlfriend.

A small part of him wanted his enemy to catch him in his sister's bed. Sweet revenge. But he hadn't developed a close enough bond with her yet that she'd choose him over her brother.

He'd been reconsidering the original plan of getting her to fall in love with him only so he could dump her and break her heart. Having Hope pick him instead of Steven would be even more satisfying.

Then he'd dump her.

Eventually.

When the time was right.

Maybe.

****

Hope

She'd shut the alarm off on her Fitbit, got up to let Lola out, then came back and snuggled next to Evan's warm body with the intention of waking him gently. Instead, she'd fallen back asleep.

The next thing she knew, Lola and Ralph—Whitney's dog that Hope had met earlier in the week, were barking excitedly.

Oh no, no, no! She knew she should have made Evan leave last night! But it'd felt so nice lying next to him that when he said, "Just let me stay," it'd been easy to agree—with the caveat that he by gone way before Steven came home in the morning.

Then she shut off her alarm, so unfortunately, she had no one to blame but herself for Evan being in her bed right now.

She tiptoed naked across the floor to click the lock on the door leading to the hall, then went in search of her robe in the bathroom.

Hope had just tied the terrycloth belt tight around her waist when she noticed Evan starting to stir.

After giving him strict instructions to stay put and be quiet, she slipped out the door and headed toward the kitchen, where she found Whitney packing up Lola's dishes and food.

"Good morning. I'm sorry if they woke you—they're happy to see each other." Whitney nodded to the two dogs still chasing each other around the house.

Hope headed to the coffee maker, looking around for her brother as she poured a cup of coffee.

"Hi. No, I was—I was awake. Um, are you guys still headed to the Cape?"

"Yeah, we just stopped to pick up Lola and a bag for Steve."

That was a relief. If they were staying, she had no idea how she'd sneak Evan out the door.

"So, are you leaving soon?"

The sooner, the better.

"I think once he gets out of the shower. Did you need him?"

"No!" she quickly exclaimed. "I mean, I'm going back to bed, so, no." Hope shuffled toward the door. "Okay, well, tell Steve goodbye for me. Have a great time—I'll see you when you get back." She paused. "You're coming back tomorrow night, right?"

"Yeah, unfortunately I have to work on Monday."

"So, not during the day or anything."

Whitney cocked her head. "We aren't planning on it."

Hope knew she was acting suspicious but couldn't help it.

She nodded her head. "Good, good. You both deserve some time away, even if it's just overnight." She took a sip of her coffee, trying to appear nonchalant. She knew she was failing, so without waiting for Whitney to respond, said, "Well, have fun," over her shoulder as she made her way back to her bedroom.

Hope leaned against the door and took a deep breath while remembering to push the lock.

Crisis averted. Hopefully.

She walked over to the bed where Evan was sitting with his back against the headboard, watching her with a cocky smile. His bare chest was mouthwatering, along with his muscular arms. Those arms that she'd slept in last night.

Hope handed him the mug of coffee. His eyes were fixed on her as he took a sip while she dramatically untied her robe and let it slip down until her shoulders were exposed.

He mouthed, "Yes!" and she smiled at the lust in his eyes when she dropped the heavy fabric in a heap on the floor and stood naked before him.

Evan set the coffee mug on the nightstand next to him, flipped the covers next to him back, and reached for her.

"Come here," he whispered as he tugged her onto the bed. "You are so fucking beautiful."

Hope put a finger to his lips and pressed her own lips together to keep from squealing when he tugged her legs until she was lying flat on her back on the bed with her legs spread wide.

With a naughty grin, he dipped his head between her thighs and swiped his tongue along her seam.

She grabbed the pillow Evan had slept on and pressed it against her face as she moaned into it. It smelled like him.

He was playing dirty. Apparently, the thought of her brother catching them naked in her bedroom amused him.

It was *not* amusing.

But she wasn't so upset about his antics that she stopped him. Instead, she tugged on his hair and pulled his face closer so she could grind her pussy on his tongue.

The bastard flicked her clit rapidly and pressed a finger inside her.

"Oh my god!" Her cries thankfully muffled by the down-alternative pillow.

"Hope?" Her brother's voice, followed by a soft knock, made her remove the pillow from her face and lift her chest off the bed to look at the door; her hand on Evan's head stilled his movement. Otherwise she thought he would have kept going.

Steven's voice called her name again from the other side of the door.

Holding her breath, she strained to look at the door handle to see if she'd pushed the lock in, almost at the exact same time it started to jiggle.

Whew. I did.

"I guess I'll talk to her tomorrow night." Her brother's voice faded as he walked away, asking Whitney, "Ready to get going?"

The sound of the front door closing had Hope letting out a big breath as she dropped back onto the bed. She lay there for a second before dramatically fluttering her thighs wider and pressing the back of Evan's head to bring him closer to her pussy.

"You may continue," she said regally.

He barked out a laugh, but resumed his ministrations, licking and fingering her until she was spasming on the bed while calling out his name.

He didn't relent until she squeezed his ears with her thighs. When he looked up at her with a grin, his face was coated in her juices.

"Good morning." She happily sighed. "What a great way to start my day."

He crawled up along her side. "I couldn't agree more."

She rolled over to lay her head on his chest and traced her finger along his collarbone.

"Can I reciprocate?"

Evan grabbed her hand as it traveled down his body on its way to his cock.

"Later, after we move your stuff into storage. Right now, I want to take you to breakfast."

Hope blinked at him, unsure if she should be offended. "So, you're choosing breakfast over a blow job?"

He released her wrist and stroked her hair. "Oh, you'll be sucking my cock, socialite. Just later. I'm choosing breakfast *and* a blow job." Then his hand stilled, and he grabbed a fistful of her hair. "You know what? Fuck later. You can suck my cock in the shower. Now."

Chapter Twenty

Hope

There was just something about doing filthy things in the shower. Maybe it was the irony.

But when Even painted her face with his cum while she sat on the shower bench, she felt her pussy getting wetter. Then, when he smeared it around her skin with the tip of his cock, she was drenched.

"Such a pretty slut," he'd said as he watched her clean his cock with her mouth.

Hope loved being his pretty slut, or better yet, his dirty little secret. They were going to have a discussion about that at breakfast.

"We need to establish some ground rules if we're going to keep doing this," she said as they toweled off.

"I'm not a big fan of rules." He smirked as he wrapped his towel around his waist.

"Too bad."

****

Evan

"Should we drive separately? In case we run into anyone you know?" she asked as they were getting ready to leave the condo.

"I think we'll be okay. It's breakfast."

"Yeah, exactly. Usually a meal shared by two people who spent the night together."

"If we run into anyone from the hospital, we'll improvise."

Hope looked at him skeptically, but didn't say anything as she gathered her purse and phone. He wrapped an arm around her waist as they walked outside. "It'll be fine. Relax."

She twisted out of his embrace and looked around. "Rule Number One: No PDA."

"That might be a hard one, socialite. You're fucking irresistible in those yoga pants."

Biting back a smile, she tried to sound stern when she said, "What'd I say about being charming?"

He ran his hand along her backside as he leaned in to whisper in her ear, "Get used to it, baby."

"I think that would be a very bad decision on my part."

"Why?"

"You know why. We've discussed this a million times. Maybe if you told me what you and my brother are feuding about..."

"I already told you—ask him."

"I did. He says you're holding a grudge because he beat you out for the ER director position."

He felt his eyebrows go toward his hairline. "*That's* what he told you?"

"That's what I just said. Is it not true?"

Evan opened his passenger door for her. "No. I couldn't have cared less about getting his job. The only reason I even applied for it was because he wanted it. There's a lot more to why I despise him than a stupid job."

"Despise is a pretty strong word."

"It's accurate, though."

She was quiet for the rest of the ride to the restaurant. Maybe he should just tell her why he hated her brother. Evan was confident then she'd understand his animosity. Maybe she'd even share it with him.

He needed to get Olivia's permission first before saying anything more.

Reaching for her hand, he said softly, "I liked waking up next to you."

Hope tugged her hand back. "You liked the idea of sticking it to my brother."

She was far too astute for her own good. Or maybe, for his own good.

"I promise you—my reasons are valid."

With pursed lips, she turned to stare out the window at the passing buildings. "We really need ground rules," she murmured wistfully.

Maybe they did. For his sake, as well as hers.

Chapter Twenty-One

Evan

"Like I said—Rule Number One: No PDA." She was sitting in the diner booth and actually logging her "rules" into a notepad app on her phone in between bites of her breakfast.

"I'll try to abide by that at the hospital, but can we be a little more lenient outside of work?"

"First of all—there's no 'try' while we're at work. And secondly, no leniency anywhere. We need to practice utter discretion when it comes to"—she gestured back and forth across the table between them—"whatever this is called."

That made him curious. "What would you call it?"

"I don't know? A dirty little secret? Scratching an itch? Enemies with benefits?"

That stung. "You think we're enemies?"

Her face softened. "Well, no. At least not anymore."

Evan theatrically rubbed his stomach. "Who taught you to throw a punch like that?"

She grinned. "Steven."

Of course he did.

However, he needed to remind her of the repercussions of what she'd done.

"It was hot how you begged me though. On your knees, pleading to suck my cock. Totally worth it."

Leave it to her to beat Evan at his own game. "It *was* hot, wasn't it?"

"Rule Number Two..." He motioned to her stylus so she'd start writing. "I'm the boss."

Her hand had been poised to write down his edict, but instead of scribing his dictation, she looked over at him. "When we're naked, and only because I like it when you are."

"So put an asterisk by it, but either way, I'm still the boss."

Hope regarded him skeptically, but wrote it down. Not glancing up, she continued her scribbling. "Rule Three: No dating."

"Each other, or other people?"

That made her stop and look at him.

"Each other. But, if we date other people—sex is with a condom only, for everyone. And getting tested is a must."

"How about we just say no dating, period. It'll make it easier."

"I can agree to that—for now."

Oh, they were going to be dating—each other, if she wanted to use semantics to call it something else, more power to her.

"Rule Four," he continued with a cocky grin as he stole a bite of her pancakes. "Your pussy is available to me whenever I want it."

She set her stylus down and cut more of her pancakes with the side of her fork. "Unless I'm working or already have plans."

He wasn't expecting her to acquiesce to that one so easily. "Fine."

"Rule Five," she said as she took another bite, then exchanged her fork for the writing utensil. "Your cock is available to satisfy me whenever I want it."

"Unless I'm sewing someone closed, of course."

"Obviously if you're working, the rule doesn't apply."

"Or already have plans," he pointed out the stipulation she'd applied to Rule Four.

"No. I get to decide if your other plans are worthy of not being available to me."

"So does that mean I get to deci—"

"Nope." She didn't even let him finish.

"That hardly seems fair."

"I don't think you can be objective enough to decide what's worthy."

She probably wasn't wrong. "Fine," he bit out.

"Rule Six..." Hope continued.

"It's my turn."

She stopped and gave him an irritated look. "Go ahead."

"I don't have one yet. Give me a second to think of one."

"*Rule Six*," she resumed emphatically with an eye roll. "No one can know about us. No. One."

"Are you telling me that you haven't told any of your friends in California about me?"

Her half smile-half grimace told him the answer.

"But she's my best friend, and she lives in California."

"So, she's not the one coming to visit over the Fourth?"

"Well..." she said with a wince.

"Then I get to tell my best friend. And my sister." She pursed her lips, so he added, "It's only fair."

"Okay, I'll agree to your best friend, but not your sis—"

Evan cut her protests off with, "You know damn well you're going to tell at least one of your sisters about me."

Her scowl let him know he was right, as did the way she stabbed at her stack of pancakes and grumbled, "Fine."

He couldn't wait to have beers with Tyler. But first, he needed to check in with Olivia and make sure she was okay with Evan *spending time* with her baby's paternal aunt.

"Rule Seven: We can mutually agree to alter any of these rules, at any time."

"Agreed," she said while she scribbled furiously. Turning the phone to face him, she handed him her makeshift pen. "Sign here."

He took the stylus from her with an amused look. "Is this our relationship agreement? Can I call you Sheldon?"

"As history has proven, you can call me pretty much anything you want," she mused. "I guess you could say this is our sexual relationship agreement."

Evan signed it without even reading it and handed her back her phone.

"Isn't that illegal?" he teased.

"I think only if money has changed hands. We're not exactly trading favors for sex."

He cocked his head with a grin. "Aren't we though?"

She didn't return his grin. "Not monetary."

With a flourish, she signed it, punctuating her signature with a tap of the electronic pen.

"I'll email you a copy. What's your private email address?"

"You don't want to send that through the hospital server?" he teased.

This time she did smile. "I think that'd be a bad idea."

He rattled off his personal email address and heard a ding on his phone a few seconds later, indicating he had a message.

"Did you decide on a storage unit?"

"I haven't even looked."

"Speaking of sexual favors for monetary value... I have a pretty big storage room in my basement that I hardly use. You're welcome to keep your things there. They'd be safe—barring a massive flood."

"As appealing as being sexually indebted to you is... I couldn't possibly impose on you like that."

"It's not an imposition, Hope. Your boxes would be in my basement storage room, out of my way. And I like the idea of you being sexually indebted to me, too."

She stared at him, obviously trying to come up with a reason why it was a bad idea. "What if I need to get something and you're not home?"

"Just call me. I'll unlock the door with my phone."

"What if you're in the middle of working on a patient and I really, really need something?"

What on earth could she possibly "really, really need" that she would have left in a box in storage? Still, he played along.

With a shrug, he replied, "I'll give you the keycode, so you can go over whenever you need to—day or night."

She still hesitated, so he said, "I was just offering. You won't hurt my feelings if you want to put your belongings in a storage unit. You know, where anyone can break in and steal your stuff."

"I think they have cameras and security."

"Suit yourself."

"Okay, fine," she sighed. "I'll use your storage room."

"Don't do me any favors," Evan muttered as he took the last bite of his omelet.

She set her silverware on her plate and looked sheepishly at him from across the table. "That was so rude. I'm sorry. Thank you—it was generous of you to offer space in your storage room for me to store my things, and you're right—I acted like I was doing you the favor instead of the other way around."

He winked at her. "It's okay, socialite. I'm sure I'll find a way you can make it up to me."

She ran her toes along his calf. "So, what kind of rent are we talking here?"

"Oh, I have a few ideas."

"I'll bet you do."

"Why don't we head back to the condo and get the first load, then I'll tell you what I have in mind for *my* load."

Hope gave him a coquettish smile and moved her foot higher so she was rubbing his balls over his pants with her toes.

He grabbed her foot and adjusted it so it was lined up with his chubby cock.

"Don't trust me?" she asked with a smirk.

"I trust you. As a matter of fact, I'll even let you suck on them later. This is just more comfortable."

They sat like that as they finished their coffee and talked about work. It was nice having someone to talk to about the hospital who he didn't feel like he was competing with. Which was almost always a given with any other doctor he dated, i.e. fucked. And the nurses were always trying to one-up him with how much more they did for the hospital than doctors. It'd been why he quit dating, per se, and opted for just having sex without the pretense of dinner and a movie, or some other shit that was meant to prolong their time together before they got naked.

But he found himself wanting to *date* Hope. Maybe it was because of her insistence that was exactly what they weren't going to do, but he realized that spending time with her when she wasn't riding his cock was proving to be *almost* as enjoyable as when she was. They were just going to have to couch it as something other than "dating."

"Rent payment" might work.

Chapter Twenty-Two

Hope

Evan's storage room was neat and orderly and, just like he'd said, hardly used. Between the Mercedes's spacious trunk, back seat, and even front seat, and her Tesla, they were able to transport more than half her unpacked boxes in one trip.

"About that rent payment..." He growled, grabbing a fistful of her hair and tugging her down to the storage room floor with him.

She happily paid her first installment.

****

After cleaning up in the half bath in the basement an hour later, she pulled on her leggings and said, "I should probably get going."

He furrowed his brow. "Why? You still owe me dinner."

"I owe you dinner? I just paid my bill."

"Noooo... you paid rent for the space. You owe me dinner for helping you *move* your boxes. Totally different."

She couldn't hide her smile. "It is, huh? Well, what was breakfast?"

His expression and tone suggested that her question was silly. "Breakfast."

She wasn't in a hurry to go back to the empty condo and watch TV alone while eating leftover takeout, so she didn't rush to disagree with him, as was always her initial instinct when it came to Evan.

With eyes narrowed, she asked, "What do you have in mind?"

"It's up to you. We can order in or get dressed up and go out. I can show you around the city."

"Going out sounds fun in theory, but I'm kind of tired and not in the mood to get ready then go out and *people*."

He laughed at her use of the word people as a verb. "Raincheck then. We'll stay in tonight."

Raincheck? As in—there was going to be another opportunity in the future?

"I feel bad—you stayed in with me last night. I'm sure you'd rather go out. It's your night off for goodness' sake."

"Why would I want to go out when I can stay here with you?"

She shouldn't like being his first choice this much.

"I'm pretty boring."

One corner of his mouth went up. "Oh, socialite, you're anything but boring."

"You can only fuck me so many hours of the day. The rest of the time…"

"You're fascinating. And brilliant. And sassy."

His declaration made her toes curl. *Dammit.*

"There you go with that charm again. What'd I tell you about that?"

"I'll work on it," he said with a smirk as he guided her toward the stairs. "Are you hungry?"

They hadn't eaten since breakfast, and it was almost six. "Starving."

"Do want tacos again?"

They were pretty damn good tacos, but still...

"No, you wanted Italian last night, let's get it tonight."

They sat on his living room couch and looked at the menu of the local Italian eatery before placing a delivery order on an app on his phone. They got enough food to feed them for days. She also noticed he paid, waving her hand away when she tried to give him her credit card.

"I thought I was buying?"

"Why would you think that?"

"Because the whole purpose of me staying is because you said I *owe* you."

"I guess you'll still owe me, then," he said with a grin.

"This isn't a date," Hope grumbled.

"Of course, it isn't. Rule Number Three clearly says no dating. That would be against the rules."

"It feels like a date."

"Well, it isn't. You said so yourself."

****

Evan

It was so a date.

He felt pretty cocky that she didn't even last a day without breaking her own rule.

This might be easier than he thought.

Should he be alarmed at how easy it was for him to play along?

Chapter Twenty-Three

Evan

"How do we keep waking up in the same bed together?" came a groggy voice next to him.

The voice that belonged to the round ass that was nestled against his morning wood, like it belonged there.

"Well, yesterday was an accident." Evan's voice was scratchy from sleep and he cleared his throat. "I'm still not sure how we both missed the alarm. And this morning can be blamed on the bottles of red wine we had with dinner last night."

The bottles of red wine that had them laughing and talking all night long. They didn't even fuck again, just fell asleep with his arms around her—her back to his front, while he breathed in the scent of her floral shampoo.

All part of the plan. He wasn't *really* getting attached to her.

"Are you hungry? I can make pancakes or omelets—those are your choices. Or cereal."

Making her breakfast in his kitchen was just part of the act, too. Nothing more.

So was kissing her messy hair before rolling over and heading to the bathroom, then going downstairs.

She appeared in the kitchen not long after he did with her smooth hair, like she'd run a brush through it.

"Pancakes two days in a row? I haven't been this spoiled since I was home on break from college. My mother loves to cook—especially breakfast."

"I'm sure I'm not nearly as good a cook as your mom, but I can hold my own. At least when it comes to simple things."

Hope peered over his shoulder at the pan on the stove. "They look good to me."

That made him smile as he flipped the flapjack.

"We can move the rest of your things today, if you want. As long as we're done before four. I'll need to get a nap in so I'm ready for my shift tonight."

"That would be great." Hope plopped down on one of the barstools at the kitchen island. "My tab's going to be huge, but I'm not taking a Sunday afternoon nap with you. It's bad enough we're spending the morning together."

"You weren't invited—I'll need to sleep and that won't happen if you're in bed with me. And what do you mean, *bad enough*? I thought our weekend was both productive and pleasurable."

"Oh, it was. Thank you. Way more productive for me, but I'm grateful for your help."

"I know." He smirked. "You showed me just how grateful a few times."

"*My point is*," she continued emphatically, ignoring his comment. "We can't date. My brother would never forgive me for..."

"Sleeping with the enemy," Evan supplied. "But we aren't dating—just fucking. We don't even like each other, right?"

"It was a lot easier when we didn't."

He huffed out a laugh. "I don't know. I think I might have fallen in love with you when you socked me in the gut."

It was supposed to be a sarcastic remark, yet it didn't feel like a lie as he said it.

The fact that she took zero shit was sexy as hell. And it turned him on when she dished whatever he gave her right back at him.

But she was the sister of the man who knocked his own sister up. How could she be anything more than a pawn in his plan to get even with Steven without it being a slap in the face to Olivia?

She couldn't be.

And yet, this had been the best weekend he'd had in as long as he could remember.

With a fake smile, she said sweetly, "There's plenty more where that came from."

"Careful, socialite. Next thing you know, we'll be ring shopping."

"Oh my god. Could you imagine? My brother would disown me. And probably the rest of my family would, too. Especially Ava."

Her words packed their own punch. He'd been so focused on how Steven would be affected when their affair became public, he'd overlooked how it would impact her.

Aw, hell. Now wasn't the time to grow a conscience.

****

Hope

"These are so good," she said, gesturing with her fork to the stack of fluffy pancakes on the plate in front of her. "Way better than I could have done. I always burn them—especially the first one. Your first one was as good as all the others."

"I'm glad you like them. I'll make them for you anytime, socialite."

"You know I'm not really a socialite, right?"

"No, I had no idea."

She dragged a bite through the syrup on her plate. "My mom is—so I take it as a compliment, by the way, but I never had a coming out party or anything."

"It was never meant to be an insult. And that surprises me."

Hope felt her eyebrows quirk. "Why?"

"I don't know. You have a refined air about you. I noticed it the first day on the elevator when you were in your Chanel suit."

She let out a laugh. "My mother would kiss you if you said that in front of her. She bought me that suit. Apparently, the cotillion classes she made us all take paid off."

"All of you? Even your brother?"

"Even Steven." She giggled at her unintentional rhyming. "Probably *because* of Steven. My mom noticed such a difference after he and Ava took the classes in middle school, that the rest of us had no choice when we were old enough."

"They worked. You are a lady, no doubt. No one would ever guess all the dirty things you like me to do to you behind closed doors."

"Let's keep it that way."

"Of course," he replied with a smirk. "Rule Six, remember?"

A thought occurred to her. "I'm not the only one who likes that, am I? I mean, you do, too, right?"

He stared silently at her for a beat. It unnerved her not knowing what he was thinking, and she anxiously pushed her food around her plate.

Finally, in a low voice, he murmured, "If syrup wouldn't be so hard to clean up, I'd sweep these plates onto the floor right now and fuck you on this counter to show you how much I like what we do."

With a seductive smile, she moved the butter and bottle of syrup to the side, then grabbed both their plates as she slid off the barstool and walked them to the sink. Turning to face him, she cooed, "Problem solved."

CHAPTER TWENTY-FOUR

Evan

Work was busier than ever. They were already had one less doctor and the influx of patients wasn't slowing down. Still, he came in early to finish showing Hope around and introducing her to the staff, but they didn't even have time to mess around afterward. Everyone in the ER was working without a day off, and Evan's schedule was crazy and sporadic. It seemed like he was working all night and going home just as the sun was coming up, only to sleep and come back to do it all over again.

Normally, he wouldn't have minded, but he hadn't seen Hope in almost five days. The only contact they'd had since finishing their tour was flirty texts and the occasional dirty picture she'd send him when he demanded it.

He might have felt bad about insisting he had if every picture of her pussy didn't show her wet. His kinky girl seemed to like it as much as he did. And he deleted them, as promised. The only one he kept was the one he'd taken the night in his living room, and she knew he had it.

He sent her a text the Sunday night before the Fourth of July weekend.

Evan: Don't take this the wrong way, but I fucking miss you.

He knew she wouldn't like him saying that. Still, she replied right away.

Hope: I think what you meant is, I miss fucking you.

Evan: That too.

Evan: Parker hired some floating docs for the weekend so some of us can be off over the holiday. I think he's worried we're going to burn out and quit on him. When does your friend get here?

Hope: Thursday.

Evan: And you're still going to the Cape?

Hope: Yes.

Evan: Any chance you'd be able to sneak away while you're there? Olivia invited me to come stay this weekend at a house on the beach she's renting.

Hope: I'm sure I could. Yvette would cover for me. But she'll probably want to meet you in exchange for her help.

That made him smile. He wanted to meet her friends. And he wanted to introduce her to Olivia. After he talked to his twin, of course. He still hadn't told her he was dating Steven's sister. He was worried she'd know something was up and interrogate him like only she knew how.

Evan: I guess that's not against the rules.

Hope: I guess not, even though I don't like it.

Hope: And don't take this the wrong way, but I was hoping to see you before this weekend. A girl has needs, you know.

That made him laugh out loud.

Evan: I have the late morning/afternoon shift Tuesday and Wednesday. Wanna have a late dinner and spend the night Tuesday?

Hope: We really should have made no sleepovers a rule.

Evan: But we didn't, so, is that a yes?

She sent back an eye roll emoji.

Hope: I guess.

He only fist pumped because he needed a good fuck. It had nothing to do with wanting to talk to her in person. Or smell her skin. Or feel her next to him.

Anything like that he was feeling was just because it was part of the plan.

Keep telling yourself that, buddy.

Why did his conscience have Tyler's voice? Evan hadn't even told Tyler he was "not dating" Hope—he hadn't had an opportunity to.

He needed to find time to talk to his friend this week. And to his twin.

He decided to push his luck with Hope.

Evan: Is Steven still staying at his girlfriend's? I could come by in the morning before you go to work.

Hope: No, he's been coming home most days this week. His gf works days like a normal person and Lola is here.

Evan knew her brother had been working as much, if not more, than he had been, so it didn't surprise him. He also didn't miss her "like a normal person" dig.

Evan: Normal is overrated.

Hope: See you Tuesday.

He was looking forward to it. To get laid, of course. No other reason.

Chapter Twenty-Five

Hope

She was seeing Evan tonight; there was no reason that she should be looking around the cafeteria for any sign of him. But anytime a dark-haired man in scrubs or a white lab coat walked through the cashier line and into the seating area, Hope was doing a double take to make sure it wasn't him.

And, truth be told, she wasn't a fan of the cafeteria and hadn't eaten there since she found out he was sleeping during the day. UberEats had a much better selection. Yet, here she was, sitting in the uncomfortable booth, slowly eating a sandwich while reading the news on her phone. Or at least trying to look like that's what she was doing.

A few people that she'd been introduced to while on her tour with Evan stopped by her table and said hi. One handsome neurologist lingered, as if waiting for an invitation to join her.

She didn't offer.

What was wrong with her? Evan wasn't her boyfriend. There was no long-term potential with him. She should be having lunch with good-looking doctors and going on dates with them.

Yet, she had absolutely zero interest in spending time with anyone but Evan.

The sex is really good, she tried telling herself. Except even she was no longer buying it. It wasn't that the sex wasn't phenomenal—it was, but there was more to it, and she knew it. And that was a problem.

After finishing the last bites of her lunch without any sign of him, she returned her tray and headed back to her office, feeling a little disappointed.

That's silly. I'm going to see him tonight!

But when she rounded the corner of the hallway leading to her office and saw him coming toward her, she broke out into a big smile and had to will herself not to run to greet him.

"Hey stranger," he said with a warm smile. "I was just coming by to see if you had time for lunch."

"Oh." The disappointment evident in her tone. "I just had lunch."

His eyes twinkled. "Did you have dessert?"

Her lips turned up into a grin. "I didn't. I think I might have something in my office though."

He returned her grin. "Lucky that I ran into you then."

Very lucky indeed.

****

Evan

He had his hands in her hair and was pushing her against the wall the second the lock on her office door clicked.

Pausing to look at her beautiful face, he lowered his mouth and kissed her for the first time on the lips.

They'd carefully avoided that before, as if both realizing it was too intimate for what they were supposed to be doing.

Evan no longer gave a shit about that. He wanted to feel his lips against hers. Explore her mouth with his tongue. Taste her moans as they mingled with his.

Her lips were soft. The taste of her lipstick blended with a mint flavor as his tongue sought out hers. Hope returned the kiss without hesitation, her hands snaking around his neck and pulling him closer with a whimper.

He was hard and pressed his clothed cock against her covered pussy. He wanted more—so much more, but the tease was both tortuous and thrilling as he ravaged her mouth.

A buzzing noise brought him back to reality, and he pulled away, trying to figure out where the sound was coming from.

Hope touched her Fitbit, and the noise stopped.

"Shit. I have a meeting with Parker in five minutes."

"Call his secretary and tell her you're running late."

"You know Parker. He'll be knocking on my door if I'm not on time before even checking with her."

That sounded like the chief of staff.

Evan let out a sigh through his nose and took a step back, trying to calm his dick down.

She reached up and swiped his mouth with her thumb, saying, "You've got lipstick all over your face."

After a few wipes, she gave up and handed him a tissue.

"Yours isn't any better," he teased as he looked at the smeared mauve surrounding her mouth.

Pulling out a mirror from her bottom desk drawer, she rubbed lotion on the stained skin, then wiped it with a tissue. He was amazed at how easily it came off.

"Can I have some of that?"

She smiled and dabbed the cool liquid on his face, then helped him clean it off.

She patted his shoulder before tossing the tissue in the trash. "There. Good as new."

"They teach you that in cotillion classes?"

"As a matter of fact…" she retorted with a wink.

Evan watched as she carefully reapplied her lipstick and ran a brush through her hair. A minute later, she looked like she did when he ran into her in the hall: fucking beautiful and perfectly put together.

He stood with his hand on the doorknob. "I should be home around seven. Cross your fingers there are no catastrophes. You're welcome to come over anytime. I'd love it if you were there when I got home. We can have dinner delivered, or we can go out."

"Let's do delivery. I'm sure you'd like to relax."

"With you sitting on my face."

She gave him a devilish grin as she closed her bottom desk drawer. "That can be arranged."

His dick, that had finally calmed down enough that he could leave without a tent in his pants, moved. He needed to get out of here before he got them both fired, so he opened the door and glanced into the hall to find no one around.

"I wouldn't hate it if you were naked when I walked in the door either."

She breezed past him and tsked. "So demanding."

Evan murmured in her ear as she locked her office, "You'll see how demanding tonight," making her fumble as she tried removing the key from the doorhandle. His ego loved it. With a subtle pinch to her ass, he murmured, "See you tonight, socialite. Seven o'clock. Be waiting for me."

"Text me if you're going to be late."

"What? No argument or sass. I should've kissed you sooner."

"Please," she said as she walked down the hall. "You love it when I'm sassy."

Yeah, he did. But he also loved it when she was submissive. He couldn't think of a damn thing not to love about her.

Except her brother.

And therein lied the problem.

CHAPTER TWENTY-SIX

Hope
She couldn't believe she was actually going to his house before he got home. Or that in her overnight bag was the sexy black bustier and thigh highs that had sat in her drawer in California with the price tags still on them. She'd been looking for a reason to wear them. The black stilettos had only been worn once.

Hope wasn't sure if she was hoping to be punished for not being naked like he requested when he walked in the door, or if she wanted him so turned on by her appearance that he'd forget she was supposed to be nude.

He'd sent her a text before she left the condo and told her to bring her toy. Hope wasn't sure what he had planned, but his previous threat of fucking her ass at the same time he used a dildo in her pussy flashed in her mind, so she didn't argue. That was a punishment she could get behind.

Hope: Any particular one I should bring?
Evan: You have more than one?
Hope: I have several. Don't judge me. I told you, I went through a dry spell.

Hence, the lingerie that was still donning the price tags.

Evan: Bring them all.

She'd never been with someone that she was so compatible with. Sexually. Just sexually.

The fact that he not only appreciated her biting wit but gave it back, or that they could talk for hours without running out of things to say, or could sit in quiet and not have it be awkward, was irrelevant.

Right?

The obnoxious sound of a wrong answer game show buzzer went off in her head. *Wrong.*

She needed to cool things off with him. Maybe suggest they should see other people. After the Fourth. No sense ruining the weekend.

****

Evan

The first thing he noticed when he walked in the door of his brownstone was the pleasant smell. The second was all the lit candles. He easily deduced the two were connected.

"Hope?" he called as he set his backpack on the bench in the entry.

She didn't respond, but there was a trail of rose petals leading from the foyer to the stairs. His shadow flickered in the candlelight on the stairwell wall as he followed the floral covered route to his bedroom.

"Hope?" he called again before pushing open the bedroom door that was slightly ajar.

All he could was utter, "Holy. Fuck," at the sight before him. His cock was instantly hard.

She was lying on the bed like a goddess. Her back slightly arched off the mattress while her blonde hair fanned out on the bed. Her tits spilled out of a black corset that narrowed at the waist then fanned out right above her luscious hips. A scrap of black fabric barely covered her pussy, and her black stockings were attached by garters that extended from her bustier. A pair of black stiletto heels sat neatly next to the bed.

Evan walked toward the bed in controlled strides. Forget goddess, she was a goddamn siren.

Who was snoring softly.

CHAPTER TWENTY-SEVEN

Hope

She heard the bathroom close softly and bolted upright. Light was coming from under the door. Evan was home. At least she hoped it was Evan.

Dammit, she'd messed everything up. She had practiced sexy poses on the bed and thought she'd perfected one. He was going to be overcome with lust at the sight of her and ravage her body on the bed all night.

Then she must have fallen asleep. It wasn't her fault his mattress was so stinking comfortable.

She huffed a breath into her hand, trying to determine if she'd been asleep long enough to have morning breath. After deciding she was still in the clear, she resumed her sexy pose and waited.

Oh, maybe she should be leaning against the wall in her stilettos—CFM—come fuck me—shoes, her sisters called them. That'd be sexy. Even though Evan was six foot three, she'd gone back and forth about wearing the high heels since Hope was over six feet tall in them—the main reason they'd only been worn once. That and they weren't the easiest to walk in.

From her sexy position on the bed, she eyed the edge of the bed where the shoes were. Did she have enough time to make it to the wall and put them on before he came out of the bathroom?

She decided to go for it and hopped off the bed and attempted to scoop up the shoes in one motion, falling flat on her face with a loud thud.

Now what? He had to have heard that. Did she abort and jump back on the bed or try to still make it to the wall?

Abort! Abort! Abort! Her brain screamed.

Hope jumped back on the bed and was about to get into her pose when she realized she had the offending shoes in her hand. Leaning over the bed to put them back into place, she heard, "Well, there's a sight for sore eyes."

No!

She looked over her shoulder to see Evan leaning against the archway that led to the en suite, wearing nothing but his boxer briefs, staring at her ass with a wicked grin.

"You stole my pose," she said as she rolled over and sat up.

"I don't know." He pushed off the wall. "I kinda liked that one."

"This isn't going at all how it was supposed to."

Tracing along her pushed up boobs with his index finger, he murmured, "You're right. You were supposed to be naked. How ever am I going to punish you?"

A whimper escaped her throat as all the delicious possibilities flashed in her mind.

"I don't know."

Evan pinched her nipple. "Sir."

"I don't know, Sir."

He released her nipple and ran the tips of his fingers down her corset and over the fabric covering her pussy.

"Your panties seem to be damp, socialite. Are you thinking about being punished?"

"No, Sir."

Evan moved the fabric to the side and smeared the wetness around her folds with his fingers. "Don't lie to me. Your body will betray you."

She said nothing.

Moving to rub her clit in circles, he asked, "Did you bring your toys?"

Butterflies erupted in her stomach.

"Yes, Sir."

He removed his hand and stood tall, staring down at her. "You are fucking beautiful in that lingerie, but it needs to go."

She unclipped the garters from her thigh highs and started to roll the stockings down her legs when he stilled her hand. "Leave those on, but everything else needs to come off."

Evan sat down on the bed with his back against the headboard and a tent in his boxer briefs. Clasping his hands behind his head and crossing his ankles, he made his intent to watch her obvious.

Hope sat up on her knees and faced him, unfastening the first clasp to reveal more of her breasts. She paused and looked over at him with a challenge in her eyes.

"I'm not above tearing that off you," he warned. "And since you bought it new to wear for me, that would be a shame."

How did he know it was—? Oh, she'd thrown the price tags in the bathroom garbage, and since his housekeeper comes regularly, there wasn't any other trash in the receptacle.

"I didn't buy it for you," she corrected. "I've had it for a while now."

"But you're wearing it for the first time—for me, so it appears you did buy it for me. You just didn't know it at the time."

"Your ego is something else."

"So's my cock, and you seem to love both."

She rolled her eyes.

"Socialite, you have until the count of three to finish underdressing before I do it for you. One—"

Hope knew he wasn't bluffing, so she made quick work of the rest of the fasteners, then slipped the corset off and dropped it to the floor. Sliding onto her back so her head was at the foot of the bed, she shimmied out of her underwear and tossed them next to the lingerie. She was on display for him—naked except for the lacy stockings.

"Good god, you are gorgeous," he murmured as he shifted his position and crept along her side. His touch was featherlight as he ran his fingertips from her hips to her shoulders.

"Show me how you play with your toy."

"Which one?" She was only half-teasing. She really did want to know which one he wanted to see her use.

"Let me see the selection."

Hope pulled the wand and dildo from her bag. She'd decided to leave her rabbit and clit sucking toy at home. No need to tell him *all* her secrets.

Evan took the wand from her and examined it, pushing the power button on in the process.

"Show me how you use this."

If she hesitated, she knew she'd think about it too much and feel too self-conscious to go through with it.

Hope got on the bed next to him, took the device from his hands, and put it between her legs. Evan pulled on her knees to widen them and dipped his face closer as she maneuvered the wand around her folds and up to her clit.

She arched off the bed and let out a low moan when she felt him press a finger inside her.

A flush crept up her body, and she panted, "Evan," as she clenched her body and adjusted the vibration on her clit.

He reached up and switched the power switch to off, causing her to let out a whine.

"Not yet, socialite." He chuckled.

Standing next to the bed, he tugged on her thighs until she was situated in front of him with her legs spread. Hope was expecting him to fuck her, but instead, he handed her the dildo.

"Warm your pussy up for me."

As she slid the plastic dick inside her, he stepped to the side of his bed, opened his nightstand drawer, and pulled out a jar of something. She realized it was coconut oil by the scent when he was standing between her legs again, applying it to his cock.

He lifted her legs higher and tipped the jar like he was going to dribble some on her pussy.

"That's going to stain your comforter," Hope advised.

"I don't give a fuck."

"You really should put a towel down. It'll take two seconds."

Evan glared at her. "Are you trying to get punished more?"

"I'm just saying. Two seconds to grab a towel versus having an oil-stained comforter…"

He dropped her legs and set the jar on the low footboard.

"Fine." He walked into the bathroom.

Two seconds later, he was back with a towel.

"I know what you're doing," he said as he placed it under her backside.

"What?"

"Stalling."

Was she stalling?

"You might be right. My one and only other anal encounter didn't go so well."

That was an understatement. He rammed it in her ass; she screamed and clenched as she tried to turn over, and bent his dick in the process. There wasn't another attempt at *anything*. She went home and never heard from him again—which she was glad for.

"So why didn't you just tell me anal's a hard limit?"

"Because I don't think it is. I trust you."

The corner of his mouth turned up, and he plucked the dildo from her hand and pulled it from her pussy. "Don't be getting all mushy on me when I'm about to fuck your ass, socialite."

Tapping her hip in a gesture she recognized as *move*, she rolled off the bed. He put the jar of oil on the nightstand, pulled the comforter back, and positioned the toys so they were within reach on the side of bed, then moved the towel toward the center of the bed.

"Get in."

Hope's mind immediately went to the meme she'd seen on social media of the alien that said, "Get in, loser, we're doing butt stuff," and she giggled as she climbed into his bed.

"What's so funny?" he asked as he slid in next to her.

"I'll tell you later."

Evan pulled her against him, so she was the little spoon. She felt his cock against her ass and she giggled some more.

"You're kind of adorable when you're nervous," he murmured in her ear. She could feel his smile against her hair. "I don't think I've ever seen you like this. Not even in the elevator when you were going for your interview with the board."

"I knew what to expect. I get nervous when I don't know what's coming."

He stroked her breasts and ran his fingers along her stomach. "You didn't know what to expect the first time I fucked you."

"I had an idea that I'd like your style."

His hand skimmed lower, exploring her folds until he found her magic button. He rubbed her clit in leisurely circles as he replied, "I like your style, too."

She felt him shift, then a few seconds later, oil landed on her hip. It quickly dripped down her butt into her crack. His hand spread it from her pussy to her rosebud, then he lifted her top leg so her knee was over his.

The dildo easily slid into her pussy and she heard the whirl of the wand seconds before she felt it on her clit. She bucked her hips at the sensation, then relaxed against his frame.

"I want you to scream my name when you come," he growled in her ear.

Hope thought he was going to wait to fuck her ass until she came. Instead, she felt his cock pressing against her star as the dildo moved in and out of her and the vibrator stimulated her clit.

On instinct, she took the wand from him and he held her hip as his cock slowly breach her ring. Her body broke into goose bumps at the sensation of being full, and Evan moved the dildo in time with his thrusts.

She shut the wand off, wanting to prolong her orgasm, and she let out a long moan.

"You like being fucked in your ass while that dildo fucks your cunt, baby?"

"Yesssss," she hissed, moving her hips in rhythm with his as she threw her arm behind her to draw his face closer.

"Fuck, you feel good," he murmured with his lips on her neck.

Her nipples were hard points; her eyes closed. Evan thrust faster and Hope flicked on the wand. She knew the minute the vibrations touched her clit, she was going to come.

"Say my name," he warned as he pushed deeper inside her.

With his cock in her ass, a dildo in her pussy, and a vibrator hitting her clit, the orgasm started at her toes and crept up her body until she shook from head to toe, yelling out, "Oh my god, Evan! Yes, Evan! Yes!" as the orgasm enveloped her.

She heard his grunts, felt his fingers digging into her hips, until his ropes of cum spurted inside her and he roared, "Fuuuuuck!"

Hope had no idea how long they lay there. She felt like she was floating above her body and slowly came back to it—she wasn't sure how long that took.

Finally, she murmured, "That was the most amazing orgasm I've ever had."

He kissed her shoulder and smoothed her hair. "Me, too, baby. Me, too."

****

Evan

That had been some earth-moving kind of sex.

What the fuck was he supposed to do now?

Pretend like nothing extraordinary just happened, that's what.

Chapter Twenty-Eight

Evan

"Where does your brother think you are tonight?" he asked as they ate takeout burgers and fries in bed.

She slurped her milkshake. "He and Lola are at Whitney's tonight. But if he comes home, I'll just tell him it's none of his business."

"Is he at Whitney's a lot?"

"Probably not as much as he'd like to be," she said with a laugh. Evan tried to quell the pit in his stomach. Part of him wanted to shout and tell her what an asshole her brother is for ghosting Olivia when she's pregnant with his kid, but a bigger part didn't want to ruin things between them—not yet.

Evan still didn't know how this was going to go. He and Hope were growing closer, but they'd both kept their guard up. She knew he was an asshole and probably still suspected he was with her just to stick it to her brother, and he, obviously, couldn't fall in love with her when the goal was to dump her and stick it to her brother. Eventually. When the time was right.

"Maybe you'll meet her this weekend at the Cape," she said as she dipped a fry in ketchup. "But I swear to God if you try to sleep with her, I'm going to cut your balls off and feed them to the seagulls."

"I don't need to sleep with his girlfriend, I'm already sleeping with his sister." He smirked. Then reminded her, "Although, it's technically not against the rules."

"I'm invoking Rule Seven and amending the rules. Rule Eight: No sleeping with other people—*especially* the significant other of siblings."

"I believe Rule Seven states amendments can only happen if both parties agree."

She raised an eyebrow at him. "You have a problem with a rule about not being able to sleep with other people?"

Even an idiot knew better than to answer with an affirmative.

"No. Not at all. I have a problem with you arbitrarily making new rules without both of us agreeing, when the rule clearly states that we both have to."

Hope crossed her arms and looked at him. "So, you don't agree to not sleeping with other people?"

Oh, she was good.

"I don't want to sleep with anyone else."

Hell, he didn't even want to spend time with anyone else—even his friends. He'd much rather spend his limited free time with her.

He continued, "And I definitely don't want you sleeping with someone else."

"So Rule Eight is adopted," she said authoritatively as she wrote on the screen of her phone. A second later, the sound of an email notification emanated from his phone on the nightstand.

"An updated sex agreement, Sheldon?" he drawled sarcastically.

"Yep," she said with a happy smile as she took a bite of her cheeseburger.

I'm in love with a nut, he thought with a grin and shake of his head. Then he froze.

I mean, I'm pretending to be in love with a nut.

He wasn't really in love with her.

CHAPTER TWENTY-NINE

Hope

Yvette squealed and ran toward her the second she noticed Hope waiting in the baggage claim area.

After a long hug, the two broke apart, and her friend looked her over. "You look amazing. Having great sex regularly is definitely working for you."

Hope looked around to see if anyone heard Yvette's declaration, then smirked. "You should try it."

"I agree. I need to find my own dirty doctor."

"Maybe this week."

"That would be perfect. Some dirty sex, then I'm back to California after a week with no complications."

"You're so full of it. You're the biggest romantic I know. And my sister is Ava Sterling, so that's saying something."

"If I had Ava's love story, I'd be a hopeless romantic, too."

"Maybe you can find your confirmed bachelor and convert him this week."

"Come on. Even Ava had to work a few months on Travis."

"Actually, I think it was the other way around. He was the one who had to convince her to marry him after she got pregnant. So, that's all you need to do—find a confirmed bachelor to knock you up, the rest will fall into place."

"You shut your mouth, Hope Francine Ericson," Yvette said as she pulled her suitcase off the luggage carousel. "I think you're the one who needs to convert Dr. Dick."

Hope patted her upper arm where she'd had an injection. "No babies for me for at least two more years, and when I do finally have one—it will not be with Dr. Dick. We can't stand each other when we have our clothes on."

Hope wheeled Yvette's carry-on through the sliding doors while Yvette pushed her checked bag.

"Really? You seem like you're spending a lot of time with someone you can't stand. You can't possibly be screwing the whole time."

"It's not *that* much time together."

"That's not what it sounds like to me."

She scowled at her BFF. "Okay, fine, he's grown on me. I can tolerate being around him when he's not naked."

Yvette burst out laughing. "There's nothing wrong with liking the guy, you know."

"I can't like him. There's no future with him."

"Why?"

"He and Steven hate each other. There's no way anyone can find out about us. Steve would be so hurt, and after everything he's done for me... I just couldn't betray him like that."

"But aren't you already doing that just by sleeping with Evan?"

Hope let out a big sigh and opened the Tesla's trunk. "Yes. And I don't need to compound it by making him my boyfriend. Besides, he's not looking for anything other than sex anyway. He likes the idea of pulling one over on Steve by sleeping with his sister."

She didn't tell Yvette about Evan thinking she was Steven's wife. It was such a dick thing to do, she didn't even want her best friend to know about it. Especially since Hope continued sleeping with him afterward.

What was wrong with her?

"I need to find a therapist here," she muttered as she started the car.

****

Evan

The saltbox house Olivia had rented for two weeks was steps away from the ocean. He could see what she meant when she'd raved, "It's so peaceful here, E. You'd love it," while trying to convince him to come for the holiday weekend.

It didn't take much persuading—especially when he found out Hope was going to be on the Cape, too.

"You made it!" his twin exclaimed as she walked out the front door while he pulled his duffel bag from the trunk.

"Wouldn't have missed it," he said as he wrapped an arm around her waist and kissed her forehead. "How are you feeling? How's my niece?"

She touched her belly over her violet sundress. "She's starting to get active. Especially when I'm doing yoga. She also likes it when I sing."

"So, it's confirmed? You're having a girl?"

"Nope. I have no idea. But, I'm not calling her—or him—it."

"You're an ob-gyn... how can you not want to know what we're having?"

"*We?*"

"That's my baby, too. She's going to need a father figure in her life and that's going to be me. Deal with it."

Olivia stood up on her tiptoes and kissed his cheek. "I love you. Thank you for being there for me."

"Always, kid."

She tsked. "You're a minute older than me."

"I'm still the big brother," he said as he opened the front door. "Show me around. This place looks great."

"It is. I was lucky Dr. McDonald had a last-minute cancellation."

"This is John's place?"

"Yes, but he built a bigger house a little farther down the Cape, so he rents this one out instead of selling it. But I might try to convince him to sell to me. I love it here."

"I think Steven's place isn't far from here," Evan said quietly. "Wouldn't that be weird?"

"Steve Ericson? Oh yeah, he mentioned he got a great deal. I didn't realize it was so close to here. Why would that be weird?"

"You'd be okay with him being just down the beach from you? I mean, I guess you work at the same hospital, so..."

Olivia cocked her head. "Yeah. Why wouldn't I be?"

He gestured to her stomach. "You know."

"No. I don't."

"The baby, and him not taking responsibility."

She stared at him with narrowed eyes, as if trying to make sense of what he was saying, then her eyebrows shot up.

"You think Steve is the father of my baby?"

"Isn't he?"

Olivia started laughing. "God, no. He's not my type at all, and I'm pretty sure I'm not his type. I think he prefers blondes—with available wombs."

Evan felt the blood rush from his head.

"You mean... he's not. But the day you told me you were pregnant. I saw you with him, and you were crying. Then you told me the father didn't want anything to do with—"

"I told you that because I didn't want you judging me, Evan."

"Judge you? Why would I judge you?"

"Because I don't know who the father is—and that was by design."

"What do you mean, you don't know who the father is, 'by design'?"

She took hold of his hand and led him to the door leading to the patio. "Come on. It's time I came clean about this."

His head was swimming, and he welcomed the opportunity to sit down.

"Are you sure you're not just covering for Steven?"

"Of course, I'm not. I can't believe you would think that Steven Ericson, of all people—the guy who adores his family, would not want to be a part of his child's life."

That's what had stuck in his craw the most, and probably why he loathed the man as much as he did.

His sister poured a glass of lemonade from a pitcher on a tray sitting on the side table between them and offered it to him. He happily accepted, gulping half of it down before she'd even finished pouring her glass.

She took a sip, then said quietly, "I'm thirty-eight years old, Evan. I wanted a baby before it was too late and I didn't want to have to go through IVF. I met a man one night at a bar and we got a hotel room together. I knew I was ovulating, but I told him I was on the pill."

He felt his eyes grow wide.

"I'm not proud of it," she continued. Then, rubbing her stomach added, "But I don't regret it for a minute. I slipped out while he was asleep. I didn't want to see him again. Not because I didn't like him, but because I knew what I'd done wasn't fair. It was easier not to know his last name or his phone number."

"That's why you told me he didn't want anything to do with the baby."

"I didn't want you judging me, Evan."

"So, why were you crying in Steven's office the day you told me you were pregnant?"

"I'd come down to the ER to tell you, but you were busy. Steven saw me crying and pulled me into his office. Those were happy tears."

"So, Steven was just congratulating you?"

"Yes. I can't believe you thought—" she stopped short. "Oh my god, is that why you suddenly hated him?"

"Well, yeah. I thought he ghosted my pregnant sister."

"That explains so much. Here I thought it was because he got the ER director job and not you."

"I only applied because I wanted to try and beat him out. He was always the better man for the job. Why does everything think that I'm jealous?"

"Because that's the only thing that made sense, doofus. You two were friends, and then suddenly you were enemies. What other sane reason would there be?"

"That he knocked up my sister and wanted nothing to do with her child."

"I feel awful I didn't tell you the truth, sooner."

"Yeah, me too. Although it makes what I'm about to tell you a lot easier."

She cocked her head and waited for him to continue.

"I'm secretly dating Hope Ericson."

Chapter Thirty

Evan

"Hope Ericson? Steven's little sister—the one with the prosthetic patent?" Olivia asked as she sat up straighter.

"Yeah, the same."

"That must be difficult to navigate—given your and Steve's animosity toward one another."

"It's part of the reason we've kept it a secret."

"But you're *dating*, like spending time together regularly? Exclusively?"

"Yes, and yes."

"Wow. Well, first of all, congratulations. I honestly was beginning to wonder if this day would ever come."

"Hold on. No day *has come*." He made quotations marks with his fingers. "Slow your roll. It's nothing serious—we're just hanging out, so don't get any ideas. We're only exclusive because we agreed that if we're sleeping together, we wouldn't sleep with other people."

She nodded thoughtfully, as if digesting what he'd just told her. "But you like her?"

Evan had never thought about it so simplistically.

"Yeah. I mean, I guess I do."

"You guess?"

"Okay, yes, I do."

"What do you like about her?"

His mind immediately went to all the dirty sexy times they'd had, because, well, he's a guy. It must have shown on his face because his twin sighed and clarified, "That doesn't involve sex."

He considered her question. "Well, for starters, she's fucking brilliant. Her ideas on kinesiology are the most innovative I've ever seen. It blows me away how intuitive she is, especially without having formally studied medicine. And she's sassy as hell—she calls me on my shit, every time. Yet, she can be incredibly thoughtful and kind. I just like being around her. She makes my day better."

"But you're not serious."

"No."

"Why?"

"That's our agreement."

"Again, I have to ask—" Her eyes widened. "It's because you thought Steven and..." Olivia gestured to her stomach. "Oh, E, I'm so sorry. I wish I would have known that's what you thought. This has to have been awful—thinking there was no future with this woman because of me."

He pondered that briefly. *Had it been awful?* No. Not in the slightest.

"You know what, sis? It's actually been great. Knowing things between Hope and I could never go anywhere took a lot of the pressure off. We've been free to be ourselves and not have to worry about putting on a facade to impress each other."

"I can see how that could be appealing. So, does knowing the truth ruin things now? Does being free to take things to the next level make it lose its shine?"

He shrugged. "We'll see. I might not even say anything for a while. Finding out you've despised a guy for four months for no reason is a lot to process."

"Hope doesn't think Steven…"

"She has no idea why I hated her brother. Steven told her the same thing you thought—professional jealousy. Which is fucking laughable to think I'd be jealous of Ericson. But I couldn't tell Hope the truth without talking to you first."

"Well, I appreciate that. That's not a rumor either Steve or I need circulating the hospital. My pregnancy is already the talk at the water cooler, and that would have compounded it by ten."

That got his ire up. He didn't like the idea of his baby sister being the fodder for hospital gossip.

"Who's talking about you?"

She shrugged. "Everyone. Doctors, nurses, orderlies… you name it. A thirty-eight-year-old single doctor—an ob-gyn of all specialties—showing up to work pregnant gets tongues wagging. *Does she have a boyfriend no one knows about? Did she use a sperm donor? How is she going to do this alone?*"

"You're not alone," Evan snarled.

Olivia patted his hand. "I know I'm not."

"I can't believe you got pregnant by a guy—"

"Drop it, Evan. This is exactly why I didn't tell you."

"Does anyone else know the truth?"

"No. Just you."

"Not even Rose?" Rose was her best friend, surely she'd told her.

"No. *No one.* So, if this gets out—I'll know exactly where it came from."

"Your secret is safe with me. Hell, I thought Steven Ericson knocked you up and didn't tell a soul—not even his sister, who I'm sleeping with and thought was your baby's aunt. You know you can trust me."

She smiled. "I know I can."

"What have you told people?"

"Nothing. It's none of their business."

"What have you told Mom and Dad? It must be something good because Mom hasn't even asked me about it."

"I told her I wasn't ready to talk about it."

"And she let it go at that?"

"Why do you think I haven't told her the sex of the baby? I gave her something else to perseverate about."

"Sneaky girl. I wondered what that was all about... Wait—you 'haven't told her the sex,' does that mean you know?"

His sister gave him an evil smile but said nothing.

"Oh my god! You *do* know! And you're holding out on me!"

"Because I know you're weak, and you'll cave when Mom starts bugging you."

"Would not," he grumbled.

"Please. You'd sell me out in a heartbeat if it meant Mom would stop bothering you about it. And if she stops bothering you about that, then she'll start bothering *me* about who the father is. So, there's no way I'm telling you what I'm having."

He couldn't argue with her logic, since she was probably right. Olivia knew him well.

"Well, maybe I'll tell her about the daddy."

"Do it, and I'll tell her about Hope. *And* that it was you who dented her new car, not some drive by vandal at the mall."

"That was twenty years ago. Go ahead."

She raised one eyebrow as if that was a challenge.

"Okay, okay. Your secret is safe."

Olivia sat back with a satisfied smile. "So, when do I get to meet Hope?"

****

Hope

She and Yvette walked into Steve's Cape Cod house without knocking, suitcases in tow.

"Hello?" she called from the foyer. Lola and Ralph started barking excitedly. God, she loved those dogs.

"In the living room!" a voice called.

They walked into the room with the floor-to-ceiling windows overlooking the ocean. That view alone would make her want to be here all the time.

Steve was nowhere to be found, but James Rudolf, an anesthesiologist at Boston General, was standing next to the open French doors that led to the patio. The sound of the waves crashing provided a soothing backdrop.

"Hey, James. Good to see you!" She turned toward Yvette. "This is my best friend from San Diego, Yvette Sinclair. Yvette, James Rudolf."

A blush crept up her friend's cheeks as she took James's extended hand. Hope had never known her friend to be shy when it came to men. What was up with that?

She didn't have time to contemplate it further as Ralph and Lola came bounding through the doorway and straight at her at breakneck speed.

"You just saw me last night!" she scolded as she pushed them off her then knelt to scratch behind their ears—one pup in each hand. Lola squirmed and tried to kiss her face, so she adjusted her hands to keep the dog at bay—leaving herself open to a tongue swipe from Ralph.

Her brother appeared, leashes in hand. "All right, you two. Let's go outside."

"I can take them," James offered.

"I can help," Yvette quickly chimed in.

Hope glanced at her friend out of the corner of her eye. *What was up with that?* While Yvette didn't hate animals, she'd not had any growing up, so she tended to be reticent about interacting with them. Now, she was volunteering to help walk Ralph and Lola?

"Thanks," Steven replied. "I'll put your bags in my office. You guys will have to sleep on the pullout. Zach already laid claim to the guest room, and we're putting Whitney's friend in the smaller guest room."

"I'm sleeping in the hammock," James added.

Hope again noticed the way Yvette's cheeks flushed. This needed to be explored. Sleeping in the same space could aid with that. Besides, it'd be easier for Hope to sneak away if she was already outside.

"Oh, we can sleep on the patio loungers," she said. "Don't worry about us—give your office to someone else."

"You sure? You got here first."

"Positive. I'll have plenty of weekends to come visit." And she planned on doing just that.

Steve handed her the leashes and kissed her forehead. "I hope so. Have I mentioned how glad I am that you moved here?"

"I am, too. Thanks for helping make it happen."

The doorbell rang again, and her brother disappeared to answer it. Hope handed Lola's leash to Yvette, and Ralph's lead to James.

"Come on. You can let them off-lead once they're outside. They're usually good about staying close as they zoom around."

*

"Hey, let me just reply to this text really quick, you guys go ahead."

There was no incoming text she needed to reply to, but judging from the shy looks between James and Yvette, Hope needed to hang back and let biology do its thing. Or chemistry. Whatever. She just needed to stay out of the way. Maybe James was the Boston Mr. Wonderful she'd been hoping for, for her friend.

As if the universe didn't want to make a liar of her, her phone dinged with an incoming text.

Evan: Are you at the Cape yet?

Hope: Yes, just got here.

Evan: Want to accidentally run into me at the fish market in about a half an hour?

Hope: I'd love to accidentally run into you. I probably won't be alone, though.

Evan: Me neither.

Hope: See you soon.

Chapter Thirty-One

Evan

"Come on, little mama." He nudged his sister, sitting on the patio lounger. "Let's go for a walk down to the fish market and get some cod."

Olivia eyed him suspiciously over the magazine she was reading. "I thought you hated going to the fish market. Anytime I've asked you to go with me, you said it reeks."

"I mean, it does."

"Exactly. So why all of a sudden do you want to go?"

"You need the fresh air, and my niece needs the Omega threes for her little developing brain."

She turned the page, letting him know she wasn't buying it.

"Fine, you don't have to go. But if I happen to run into Hope while I'm there, it's not my fault you missed a chance to meet her."

Putting the magazine down, she sat upright. "Why didn't you just say so?"

"You're not very versed in clandestine relationships, are you?"

She put both hands on her stomach. "You mean other than the obvious?"

"Yeah, not the same."

"Fair enough."

She struggled to put her canvas tennis shoes on.

"It helps if you untie them," he teased.

"Yeah, but then I have to retie them. A feat that's getting harder and harder."

"You're not even that big yet."

"Put a pillow under your shirt and tell me how easy it is to bend over and tie your shoe."

Evan tucked one of the throw pillows next to him under his shirt and bent over to mimic tying his shoe with no problem.

"Yeah, well, your arms are longer. That plays a factor."

Pulling the pillow out with a smile, he knelt in front of her and tied her shoes. "You're right. I forget you have little T-Rex arms."

She smacked his shoulder. "You're such an ass."

"I know. Hope reminds me on a regular basis."

"You're an ass to her?"

"Every day," he said unapologetically.

The corner of her mouth turned up. "Uh-oh."

"What? You and Tyler with your 'uh-ohs.'" He stood up quickly. "There's no uh-oh."

"You're only an ass when you're teasing. And you only tease people you care about."

"You're crazy. I tease lots of people. All the time."

"No, you don't."

"Of course, I do. How would you know?"

Olivia smirked. "The lady doth protest too much, methinks."

He continued the Hamlet dialogue, "Oh, but she'll keep her word."

Olivia stood and walked past him, muttering, "We're driving, and you're annoying."

"I thought we already established that," he called before grabbing his car keys and jogging after her.

****

Hope

She walked out to where Yvette and James were on the beach, tossing the ball for the dogs. "Hey! Do you want to walk the dogs down to the fish market?"

"The fish market? You want to buy fish?" Yvette asked as she picked up the ball Ralph had dropped on her foot. "Why?"

"Well, not necessarily *buy* fish. More like... just walk around."

"At a fish market?" James asked. "Kind of a weird place to pick to want to walk around."

"It's famous. I wanted to show Yvette."

"Yeah, because living in San Diego my whole life, I've never been to a fish market," her best friend snarked under her breath as she tossed the ball.

That made James burst out laughing.

Hope looked at her colleague with narrowed eyes. Yvette's joke wasn't *that* funny.

Hmm... Seems like someone is a smitten kitten.

This was good. Yvette meeting Mr. Wonderful was vital in Hope's plan to get her friend to move closer. From what little she knew about James, he seemed like a good guy. He had a good reputation at work as being dependable and hard working—just like Yvette. He was handsome, successful, and had always been kind to Hope in their interactions at the hospital. And the lunch ladies in the cafeteria loved him, which was saying a lot because they didn't seem to like many people.

"Well, if you'd rather stick around and help Zach and Barbie build sandcastles, by all means, suit yourself. I'm going to head down to the pier. You have fun."

"No, no. I'll go," Yvette said, leaning over to clip Lola's lead on.

"Me, too." James whistled for Ralph, who came trotting up and dropped the ball at James's feet. "Good boy," he praised as he attached Ralph's leash to his collar.

The three humans and two dogs walked along the sand as they made their way to market.

"You didn't tell me it was this far a walk," Yvette groused after they'd been walking awhile.

"I didn't know, to be honest."

"We probably can't get an Uber back with the dogs, either."

"I can walk the dogs back and you ladies can get a ride," James offered.

"Don't be silly," Yvette quickly replied. "We all came together; we'll go back together."

Hope pressed her lips together to keep from smiling. The two of them were adorable together—and she hadn't even planned their meeting, it'd been completely organic. Even better.

The fish market came into view minutes before the smell hit them. Hope fought to keep a neutral face and not wrinkle her nose as they got closer. She was supposed to want to be there.

Evan, dressed in khaki shorts and a navy-blue T-shirt, and an adorable pregnant woman who bore a striking resemblance to him, walked onto the faded wooden planks of the market from the other direction the same time the three of them did.

James was the first to acknowledge them.

"Olivia! Evan!" He stole a quick glance at Hope; a smirk escaped his lips as he continued, "What a surprise."

Evan offered his fist to bump with James. "What's going on, James?"

Lola approached him; her wiggling butt made it obvious she was familiar with him. He reached down and scratched under her chin—her favorite spot. "Hey, pretty girl. How've you been?"

"We're just here to celebrate the weekend at the beach. For some reason," James paused dramatically and looked in

Hope's direction, "Hope wanted to come down to the fish market. It's such a coincidence to run into you two."

"Isn't it though?" Olivia said with a conspiratorial smirk.

"It's a small world," Hope said with a nervous laugh.

"Yeah, that's it," James replied. "Small world. Nothing planned or anything."

Evan coughed into his hand and stood, putting a protective hand on Olivia's back as he did. "Olivia, have you met Hope Ericson? She's with the prosthetics department at the hospital."

"No, but I hear your invention is revolutionary." The dark-haired beauty said with a warm smile as she extended her hand. "Olivia Lacroix. So great to finally meet you."

"Same here," Hope replied as she took his sister's petite hand.

Evan smiled politely at Yvette and stuck out his hand. "And I'm sorry, I don't believe we've met. Evan Lacroix."

"Yvette Sinclair. Nice to meet you. I've heard a lot about you."

Still holding Yvette's hand, Evan raised his eyebrows and smirked at Hope as he replied, "Oh, you have, have you?"

"I told her how full of himself my mentor doctor is."

That made Olivia chuckle then tilt her head to murmur an aside to her brother, "I like her."

He tried to look grumpy, but a slight smile escaped his lips. "Do you want to walk with us? We're going to get some cod. My niece—or nephew—needs some fish for her developing brain."

"Sure. If you don't mind. I mean, since we don't know what we're looking for," Hope said.

They walked further in, making small talk and stopping to inspect a fresh catch after being summoned over by the proprietor.

"Hope," Evan said loudly as he tugged on her elbow to lead her away from the group. "I wanted to clarify something about that patient we were discussing this week."

"Of course!"

Once they were at the railing away from everyone, he looked at her with a warm smile and simply said, "Hi."

"Hi," she said, returning his smile. "When did you get here?"

"This morning."

"Us, too."

"Too bad we couldn't have all just ridden together."

She'd never even considered it until he just said it.

"That probably wouldn't have gone over very well with Steve. Although his house is currently full, so he might not have noticed. Besides, we're heading to a B and B from here."

"That sounds like a fun trip."

"I'm looking for one I can be a silent partner in with Yvette. I put up the cash, she puts in the labor—we split the profits fifty-fifty."

"A bed-and-breakfast, huh?"

"She's a hotel manager, but her dream is to open a bed-and-breakfast. I'm trying to convince her to move here and do that. The problem is she won't take me up on my offer to front the cash. She keeps saying friends and money don't mix."

"She's got a point."

"That's what contracts are for. Besides, I don't care about the money—I'd just give it to her if she'd let me. I have more than I know what to do with."

"That's not a bad problem to have," he observed while brushing away a strand of hair the breeze had blown into her face.

"Did you two get that patient situation figured out?" Yvette's voice came from behind her.

Hope turned to find James, Yvette, the dogs, and Olivia—who was holding up a bag of what Hope assumed was fish.

"I guess we better get that home before it begins to stink," Evan said with a reluctant laugh and stepped toward his sister.

"We're having a bonfire tonight," Hope blurted out. She glanced between Olivia and Evan. "You two should swing by if you're not busy."

Evan glanced toward Olivia, who gave a slight nod of her head before he turned back and said, "Yeah, we could probably do that. What time?"

"I'm assuming when it gets dark—around nine."

He looked at his sister again. It was sweet how much he looked out for her. "Can you stay up that late, *mamasita*?"

"Yes, but I'm going to need a nap this afternoon."

Wrapping his arm around Olivia's waist, he said, "I better get this lady home then. Can you text me the address, so we don't show up at the wrong house?"

"No problem. See you tonight."

Evan paused to say goodbye to the dogs, then offered another fist bump to James and a "Nice to meet you, see you later tonight," to Yvette.

Yvette watched the pair walk toward the parking lot and sighed wistfully. "They were smart and drove."

"Come on," Hope said, hugging her friend's shoulders. "I'll buy you some ice cream, then we'll make the trek back."

"You do realize the two of you aren't fooling anyone, right?" James asked as they walked toward the ice cream shop.

"Why, Dr. Rudolf, I have no idea what you mean."

He gave her an annoyed look. "Yeah, yeah. Just be careful tonight. I don't want your brother getting into a fistfight with Evan. We can't afford to be down two more ER doctors."

"I know. I'll be on my best behavior."

The question is, would Evan?

She got her answer fifteen minutes later in the form of a text message as the three walked along the beach back to Steven's.

Evan: No underwear tonight.

Hope: You or me?

Evan: You.

Hope: That hardly seems fair.

Evan: Who said anything about fair, socialite? See you tonight. No panties, or you'll be punished.

Decisions, decisions.

Chapter Thirty-Two

Evan

"I can't believe that you agreed to go to Steven's tonight," Olivia said once they were driving back from the fish market.

"Well, I have to try to mend fences sometime. No time like the present."

"Mend fences? You're the most stubborn man I know. Never once in your thirty-eight years have I seen you try to *mend fences*."

"Well, this is the first time I've been wrong."

Olivia coughed like she was choking. "Did you just admit to being wrong? What the hell is going on with you? I might have to insist you marry this woman if she's going to have such a good influence on you."

He glanced at his sister, then back at the road. "This has nothing to do with Hope."

He looked again to find her giving him *the look*. The same one their mother gave him when she didn't believe a word he was telling her.

"What?"

"You're so full of shit your eyes should be brown."

He let out a deep sigh. "I was way off base with Steve."

"Yes, you were. But normally your pride wouldn't let you fix it."

"Maybe I'm growing as a person. Did you ever think of that?"

"Oh, you are."

"Thank you."

"Because of her."

Was that true?

"Okay, *maybe* she does have something to do with my wanting to make amends with her brother. I'd rather not worry about getting shot if he catches me with her."

Olivia's tone dripped with sarcasm. "Yes, yes. One less thing to worry about."

Evan scowled, unable to think of a snappy reply, so he gripped the steering wheel tighter and looked straight ahead. "I'm not talking about this with you anymore."

"Do you think you'll get married here or in San Diego?" she goaded, completely ignoring his comment.

"You're not funny."

"What are you talking about? I'm hilarious."

****

Hope

As they neared Steven's place, she noticed Zach and Barbie lying on a blanket in the sand by the ocean. Not far from them sat a beautiful, dark-haired woman in a beach chair while a muscular man frolicked in the surf in front of her like a ten-year-old.

"Hey, brother. Where have you been?" Zach called with his hand shielding the sun from his eyes as they approached.

"We took the dogs for a walk, trying to wear them out."

Ralph and Lola began tugging on their leashes with a whine, as if they wanted to investigate the dark-haired woman further.

She was obviously acquainted with them, calling, "Ralph! Lola! Come."

Hope let Lola's lead go, and Yvette followed suit with Ralph. The two bounded over to the lady and Hope, worried they were going to bum rush her like they usually did with Hope, started toward where she sat. Instead, once they got within licking distance, Hope heard her say, "No. Sit," and they instantly complied.

"Good dogs," the woman said and rubbed their heads.

"Wow. You're so good with them."

"We've gotten to know each other over the last month." She stretched out her hand. "I'm Zoe. I live next door."

"So great to meet you! I'm Steve's sister, Hope."

"Steven mentioned his sister was moving here. Are you that sister?"

"I am. Just got here a few weeks ago." Hope gestured to the dogs, still sitting obediently next to Zoe's chair. "They really listen to you."

Zoe chuckled. "It's because they think I have treats. I usually do when they wander over to my house."

"That's considerate of you. I know some people would get mad at having their neighbor's pets on their property."

"That's not how we do things around here. We all look out for one another."

"I know Steve appreciates having you next door. Do you and your—" She gestured toward the Adonis playing in the surf.

"Rolando is my... visitor this weekend," Zoe said with a smirk that implied next weekend's visitor would be different.

"Would you and Rolando like to stop by our bonfire later?"

"That would be fun. What time?"

Hope called to James, who was talking to his brother. "Do we know what time the bonfire is tonight?"

"Probably at dusk."

That got Rolando's attention. "We're having a fire tonight?" His accent only added to his sex appeal, but Hope got the impression there wasn't much upstairs.

Speaking of beauty and no brains, Barbie sat up and squealed, "We're having a bonfire tonight? With s'mores?" as she adjusted the strip of fabric over her implants.

Perhaps enticed by the possibility of a nip slip by the gorgeous woman, Rolando moved closer. "What are s'mores?"

James and Yvette escaped to where Hope stood. Zach quickly followed.

"Have you guys met Zoe? She's Steven's neighbor. I invited her and Rolando to the bonfire."

"No. I haven't had the pleasure," Zach butt in with an extended hand before anyone else could reply. "I'm Zach."

A slow smile crept along Zoe's face as she took his hand. "Zoe Taylor." She gestured to the empty chair next to her. "Won't you sit down?" She then turned to Yvette and James. "I don't like making assumptions, but I'm going to guess you two are brothers."

"James Rudolf. And this is our friend from San Diego, Yvette."

Their friend—interesting.

"How are you liking the Atlantic versus the Pacific?" Zoe asked.

"It will be interesting to watch the sun rise over the ocean tomorrow rather than watching it sink into the horizon."

"I'm looking forward to that, too," Hope added.

"It truly is breathtaking. I hope you get a chance to witness it while you're here."

"We're sleeping on the patio, so I hope so," Yvette said.

Zoe quirked her head. "You're sleeping on the patio?"

"All the bedrooms are taken," James supplied. "I called the hammock, and these ladies are on the loungers."

"Oh, that's nonsense when I have lovely unoccupied guest rooms."

Zach frowned from the chair next to Zoe. "Well, now I feel bad. Sending you guys next door. I should be the one to go."

"It's you and Barbie. It makes sense that you two sleep in the same bed," Hope replied.

"Oh, yeah." Had he forgotten about Barbie?

Zoe gestured to where Barbie and Rolando were playing in the surf. "It'd probably be better if they didn't sleep under the same roof."

Zach looked on at the beautiful pair. "You're probably right."

The thing that struck Hope the most was neither Zach nor Zoe seemed jealous. She understood that. Knowing that the person you were with was only temporary allowed that.

So, why then did she feel her claws come out the other day when a nurse Evan was talking with got a little too handsy—stroking his biceps and leaving her hand on his forearm until he walked away. She and Evan were only temporary.

It's because of our agreement, nothing more, she told herself.

But it was beginning to feel like something more, and that worried her. He was a self-professed player. And her brother despised him. No good was going to come from thinking this could be anything other than what they'd agreed on.

Chapter Thirty-Three

Hope

After they'd cleaned up the dinner mess, she slipped into the powder room with her makeup bag and suitcase. She removed her panties and thought about putting on a pair of jeans, but then decided they'd be too cumbersome for whatever Evan might have planned, so she pulled on a pair of yoga pants instead, along with a fresh T-shirt.

Hope ran a brush through her hair and reapplied her makeup, then rezipped her bags and stashed them back in the hall closet, next to Yvette and James's bags.

The three patio dwellers had talked about it and decided to take Zoe up on her offer to stay in her guest rooms. Although, Hope might "get lost" on her way to the neighbor's later. She was sure Yvette and James wouldn't mind. They appeared to be hitting it off. Poor Zach was suffering from a case of FOMO, not being included in the invitation. Barbie didn't seem to be nearly as appealing to him as Zoe. He'd talked all afternoon with the neighbor until Aiden came down to tell him dinner was ready. Fortunately, both Zach and Zoe were in the same boat as far as temporary companions went.

Steven disappeared moments before Zach suggested they get the bonfire going, so Zach, Aiden, and James transferred logs from a woodpile on the patio down to the firepit at the beach.

Yvette, Dakota, and Hope carried all the camping, beach, and folding chairs that were in the outside closet.

"Is that enough?" Yvette wondered out loud as she surveyed the chairs around the fire.

"We can get a couple of towels, too," Hope suggested.

Aiden snapped his fingers, as if remembering something. "I have a couple of chairs in my trunk for when I go to my kids' soccer games." He turned to Dakota. "Can you help me?"

The gorgeous hippie chick smiled and said, "Sure."

Yeah, like he needed help carrying two camping chairs.

Yvette and James, Aiden and Dakota, Steven and Whitney. Heck, even Zach and Zoe—although they couldn't do anything about it this weekend. It was the damn Love Connection around there.

That left her and Evan. And Olivia. Hope suspected there was a story with the woman's pregnancy but didn't want to ask. Plenty of women chose to be single mothers these days.

Speak of the devil, the mother-to-be came into view seconds before Evan. Evan was carrying a box of Summer Shandy beer in one hand and a six-pack of Sprite in the other.

Olivia stood to the side to let Evan make his way to the coolers. "Hey everyone!" he called as he opened the lids and deposited the beers and soda.

"Hi, guys! Glad you could make it!" James said as he got up from his chair in front of the fire and gripped Olivia below the elbow to steer her toward a green camping chair. "You need to sit down, little mama."

She gave him a grateful look and quipped, "You realize I'm never going to be able to get out of this thing on my own, right?" as she sunk into the chair.

"There're plenty of people to help you with that. Don't you worry."

Evan came to stand next to where she, Dakota, Yvette, Aiden, Steven, and Whitney were talking. Her brother and Whitney had seemed out of sorts today, but the way he now had his arms around her, they appeared to have worked it out. Which was good because Steven didn't even snarl when Evan said, "Great place you've got here, Steve."

"Thanks. It's been nice having somewhere close enough to get away when I can."

Oh my. The two men had almost been civil to one another.

Zach appeared with two beers in his hand and offered one to Zoe before he sat down next to her. The two were almost oblivious that their dates were deep in conversation. Well, as deep as Barbie and Rolando could get. Hope was pretty sure she overheard a heated discussion about hair gel.

Yvette went to sit next to Zach and Olivia, and the spotlight shifted to Aiden, which seemed to make the man uncomfortable. By all accounts, he was a brilliant cardiologist but was more taciturn in group settings outside of work. Steven told her he'd been through a nasty divorce last year that left him gun shy. Except, from what she'd seen today—he'd been nothing but sweet toward Dakota. Everyone else… not so much. That's not to say he was rude, just more reserved. Dakota seemed to bring out a softer side to him.

"What about you two?" Aiden directed his comment to Steven and Evan, trying to deflect the attention. "Your department is so short staffed; I was surprised you were both able to get away at the same time."

Steven replied, "I had a frank conversation with Parker. Until we get our new hires on board, he's bringing in floating doctors and nurses. Hell, even after the new hires are on board, we may still have to. We could easily add two more doctors and four or five more nurses, otherwise we're going to run the risk of burnout and lose people we can't afford to."

"Can your budget handle that?" Aiden asked, knowing the exorbitant rates traveling nurses and physicians could demand.

"No. Which is why we need to hire more people, asap."

"That would be great," Evan said. "Thanks for going to bat for us."

Okay. What the hell is happening here?

Steven looked as startled as she was at Evan's response. Wrapping an arm around Whitney's waist, he looked down at her with a smile. "It's entirely self-serving. I need more free time to spend with her."

Evan glanced over at Hope. His look conveyed he felt the same.

That should not make her stomach erupt in butterflies. But it did.

Whitney pulled Steven aside to whisper something while Aiden and Dakota engaged Hope in small talk. She felt Evan's finger subtly stroke her hip. She knew he was checking for panty lines.

"Good girl," he leaned in to murmur in her ear with a smirk.

Dakota shivered, and Aiden directed her toward the fire. Steven and Whitney joined them, leaving Evan and Hope standing by the coolers alone.

"Think anyone would notice if we disappeared?" he teased.

"I think so. They haven't had enough to drink yet."

"Good point."

"Yvette, James, and I are sleeping at Zoe's tonight."

"Correction. Yvette and James are sleeping at Zoe's tonight. You're sleeping in my bed. Well, I don't know how much sleeping we'll actually do, but…"

She couldn't find a reason to argue.

****

Evan

It was strange, hanging out at Steve Ericson's house—with Steve, his girlfriend, and Olivia at the same time. All the anger he'd been harboring toward his former friend was gone, replaced with… regret? Guilt? Relief? Exactly what, he wasn't sure. Maybe a combination.

Regret at ruining a friendship. Guilt over not delving deeper and being there for his sister when she needed him most. And relief that the possibilities with Hope were now unrestricted. Or they would be once he explained things to her and mended the relationship with Steve.

The night started to wear down, and Olivia looked like she was going to fall asleep in her chair by the fire.

"I need to get this mama-to-be home while she's still coherent enough to walk," Evan said with a laugh.

His sister looked up at him pathetically from her chair and held her hand up in the universal *help me up* gesture.

James jumped up and took her other hand, and the two of them hoisted her from her seat.

"I told you not to worry," their friend said with a grin.

"Thanks. I appreciate it. I need to go to the bathroom before we head back," Olivia said matter-of-factly. She tended to get curt when she was tired.

"Let me show you where it is," Hope said, and motioned her toward the house. Evan followed, waiting on the patio while the two women went inside.

A second later, Hope stepped back onto the patio. He looked over his shoulder to make sure no one was coming up the path to the house, cupped her face in his hands, and kissed her with the urgency he'd been feeling all night. Being so close, yet not being able to touch her, had been driving him crazy.

He released her and found her wearing a dazed smile with her eyes still closed. Slowly, she opened them.

"Wow. What was that for?"

"Because I've wanted to do it all night and couldn't."

"Well, it was…" She was flushed. Evan loved that he had that effect on her. "Um, a nice surprise."

"I still need to reward you for being a good girl and not wearing underwear. Although, it probably would have been easier if you would have worn a dress tonight."

"A dress to a bonfire isn't very practical," she observed.

"True. So, what time can you sneak away?"

"I'll text you when we're heading over to Zoe's. I suspect things will break up soon, now that you guys started the ball rolling."

Olivia appeared in the doorway. "Ready?"

"I am." His sister walked past them toward the patio gate, and he murmured in Hope's ear, "Don't keep me waiting long," before following after Olivia.

He felt her body tremble at that, so he wasn't surprised when he got a text from her thirty minutes later that said: **Leaving in five minutes**.

Good girl.

Evan: Where are you?

Hope: Still at Steven's. Going to walk over to Zoe's with Yvette and James, then I'll slip out.

Evan: Stay there. I'll come get you.

Hope: I'll be okay.

Evan: Stay there, socialite. I'm not kidding.

Hope: Are you always this bossy—oops, never mind. I already know the answer to that.

Evan: You're just begging to be punished, aren't you?

She sent back a winking emoji. He'd take that as a yes. Seconds later, he was out the door on his way to Zoe's beach house and the woman he could finally admit he was falling for.

Chapter Thirty-Four

Hope

Zoe showed Yvette and Hope to one guest room, and right across the hall was the one for James.

After pointing out the bathroom, where towels were, and explaining how the TV remotes worked, she said, "I'm on the other side of the house, upstairs, so don't worry about making noise. If you want to stay up and watch TV, or just hang out in the kitchen or on the deck, it won't bother me a bit. I won't set the alarm tonight. *Mi casa es su casa.*" The raven-haired beauty gave them a wink. "I'll see you in the morning." She disappeared to, Hope assumed, go have sex with her Adonis boytoy. Rolando seemed to have forgotten about Barbie when the buxom blonde sat on Zach's lap and played with the hair on the back of his neck while pushing her boobs against him.

Zoe had given Zach a knowing smile, then allowed Rolando to dote on her. It wasn't long after that, that Zoe thanked Steven and Whitney for "a lovely evening," said her goodbyes to Zach, Barbie, Aiden, and Dakota, then suggested James, Yvette, and Hope walk with her to her house so she could show them their rooms. Rolando was all over her, and she hadn't discouraged it.

More power to her, Hope thought. She'd bet money Zach and Barbie were doing the same thing. She respected how they could separate sex from emotional attachment. That's how it was supposed to be with Evan.

Supposed to be.

Maybe it was the fact that their affair was ongoing and not just a weekend fling, but she knew she'd started developing feelings for him.

That's why they needed to cool things off beginning next week. Why hadn't they made Rule Number One: No falling for each other?

It'd just be one more rule we'd break, she thought with a scowl. Rule Six appeared to be shot to hell, along with Rule Three.

Rules were in place for a reason!

Yet, she obviously didn't give a damn about any of that as she found herself saying to James and Yvette, who'd seated themselves at the kitchen table with a deck of cards, "I'm going to go back to Steven's for a while."

Yvette nodded her head with a smirk while she shuffled the deck like a card shark. "Sure, you are. Tell him we said hi."

"We won't wait up," James added with his own grin.

Hope scowled, but didn't disagree as she walked out the door. She debated disregarding Evan's demand to stay where she was and instead meet him on her way to the house Olivia had rented. She would have been more willing to be defiant, but she wasn't exactly sure which house it was and didn't want to end up at the wrong place.

It didn't matter, because he was waiting when she stepped onto the sand.

"Does Yvette know not to wait up for you?"

"Not in so many words, but I think she has a pretty good idea. Besides, I wouldn't be surprised if she doesn't sleep in our room, so she wouldn't know anyway."

"She can always text you."

Hope patted her back pocket. "Yep, I've got my phone and my toothbrush."

"Everything you'll need."

He reached for her hand with a grin as they walked along the wet sand. She couldn't help but smile back; they'd never held hands before.

"I think the salty air is messing with your brain."

He looked down at her with quizzical brows. "Why do you say that?"

"Well, first of all, you were almost friendly toward my brother tonight. And now you're bordering on being romantic—coming to pick me up, holding my hand as we walk along the sand in the moonlight. It's kind of creeping me out."

He stopped, but didn't let go of her hand. "Romance creeps you out?"

"Well, not normally. But when it's coming from you? Yes. People know I'm with you tonight, so don't get any ideas about killing me and not getting caught."

That made him laugh out loud.

"So, the only way I could possibly show you any affection is if I'm planning on killing you later?"

"Why else would you?" she replied cheekily.

"I don't know. Maybe I like you?"

His revelation made her stomach dip. Still, she replied, "Woah, woah, woah. I think there's a rule against that."

He pulled her closer and wrapped his arms around her waist. "There's not. I double-checked the rulebook." Then he lowered his face to capture her lips with his.

His lips were soft, but his mouth was cold and he tasted like mint, like he'd just brushed his teeth. Hope was glad she'd been chewing gum earlier.

What the hell was going on?

This worked between them because they couldn't stand each other, but their sexual chemistry was off the charts. He was her brother's nemesis—therefore, they couldn't be anything more than fuck enemies. They couldn't even be considered fuck buddies.

She broke the kiss. "You're complicating things. Stop it."

"How am I complicating things?"

"You're bringing feelings into this. We can't keep doing this if there's going to be feelings."

"Because I admitted that I like you?"

"Yes! You're supposed to choke me and be rough with me and call me names, not be nice to me and hold my hand or come pick me up."

He cocked his head as if confused. "And I can't do both?"

"I don't know. No, probably not. At least not in my experience."

"Might I remind you, I walked you to your car the first night I fucked you—even after you'd punched me, and you offered to drive me home the next day because I was too tired to drive?"

"Well," she sputtered. "That was different."

"And," he continued, slowly tracing her nipple over her shirt. "I made you beg to suck my cock not more than forty-eight hours later."

"Yes! I do remember, and it was hot as hell. That's what I mean. If we like each other..."

The corner of his mouth lifted. "You think just because I admit that I like you, I won't own you and make you beg?" He grabbed a fistful of her hair and tugged so she had no choice but to drop to her knees on the wet sand. "Oh, socialite. Think again."

****

Evan

If that's all she was worried about, taking things to the next level was going to be a piece of cake.

Sex with Hope was amazing. She was his fantasy woman come to life. Adventurous, not afraid to tell him what she liked and wanted, beautiful, and submissive. Yet still sassy as hell with her clothes on—and so fucking brilliant. How he ever thought he'd be able to let her go, he had no idea.

Because you never really believed it.

Oh, he'd wanted to believe it. Had even told himself it was going to happen, but deep down, he knew.

He pulled his hard cock from his shorts and slapped her face with it a few times, then used the tip to trace the outline of her mouth.

"Beg."

She looked up at him with an evil smile to let him know she wanted to play along. Her hand rubbed his thigh under his shorts.

"Please, can I suck your cock?"

He moved his hips so he slapped her face again with his dick. "Sir."

Hope grasped his shaft—her soft hands made him catch his breath—and she was the one who traced her lips this time, while murmuring, "Please let me suck your cock, Sir. I want you to use my mouth and come on my face."

The image of her face covered in his cum popped into his mind, and he groaned, "Fuck," before putting his hand behind her head and pressing gently. "Suck my cock, socialite."

She paused and looked up at him with a cocky smirk. "That's *slut* to you. Sir."

"My apologies. Suck my cock, slut."

She took him in her mouth, moaning as she did. The vibrations amplified her efforts, something he was sure she was aware of.

Then she deep throated him, and he had to close his eyes. Watching her suck him off was so fucking hot, he was going to blow his load before he wanted to.

He felt her pop his cock from her mouth, but instead of stroking his wet shaft like he was anticipating, she stopped.

"This is hurting my knees."

Evan pulled the waistband of his shorts over his cock. "Well, get up, baby." He grabbed both her hands to help her stand.

Hope eyed him suspiciously. "I don't know how I feel about the nice version of you. It feels like a trick."

He grabbed her ass and prodded her along the sand. "Well, Halloween's a long ways away, socialite, so, no tricks. Just treats."

Chapter Thirty-Five

Hope

They lay naked in the guest bedroom—the windows open so they could hear the lull of the waves crashing onto the shore and feel the breeze coming off the ocean.

Once again, Evan proved he was as dominant and dirty as ever, and she needn't worry in that department. It was him holding her in his arms and running lazy circles along her hip while they talked pillow talk that she needed to worry about.

Or when he whispered, "Where are you going?" when she got up in the middle of the night and started to get dressed.

"I need to get back."

"No, you don't. You can go back in the morning, after the sun has come up. Yvette knows where you are—you said so yourself." He patted the space next to him that she'd just occupied. "Stay with me tonight."

And she definitely should be worried about how easily she slid back beneath the sheets and into his waiting arms without an argument.

"I'm leaving as soon as the sun comes up," she warned, as if that somehow made her staying more acceptable.

Hope shouldn't feel so content snuggled next to him. Or safe.

It's just the dominant sex, she tried telling herself. After the way he'd just owned her body, of course, she felt those things. It was only natural she'd want to remain close to him, too.

****

Evan

"Baby, you need to wake up," he murmured softly in her ear.

Light was coming through the windows, and she grumbled, "It's too early," while turning to her side and putting a pillow over her head.

"Hope," he tried again, rubbing his hand up and down her upper arm while giving a soft shake. "You said you wanted to leave at dawn."

The hand that had been holding the pillow in place on her head thumped to her side, and she slowly pulled the pillow down with her other hand; blinking rapidly at him as if trying to process his words.

Then she scrunched up her face like she was about to cry and fake sobbed, "Why did I say that?" while flopping dramatically onto her back.

"You weren't lying about not being a morning person," he chuckled.

"I *hate* mornings. I was prepared to turn down Boston General's offer if they didn't agree to my 'no meetings before ten' stipulation."

"You specified that?"

"It's in my contract."

Damn. Talk about negotiating skills.

"Then why did you say you'd get up at dawn to go back?"

She narrowed her eyes at him. "Because you didn't want me to leave in the middle of the night, and you lured me back to bed with your body heat."

Evan felt his forehead wrinkle as he raised his eyebrows. "You stayed for my body heat?"

"It was chilly when I got out of bed!"

"Uh-huh, sure. My body heat. We'll go with that."

She pursed her lips, but said nothing else about it as she groused at the gods and stumbled out of bed, gathered up her clothes, then disappeared to the bathroom. While she was gone, Evan pulled on a pair of grey sweatpants and a fitted navy-blue T-shirt, then slipped his feet into a pair of slides.

"What the hell are you doing?" she asked when she reappeared.

"Walking you back to Zoe's."

She put her hand on her hip. "Wearing that? If you wanted to have sex this morning, you should have said so before I got dressed."

"I mean, I'm always up for sex with you, but I thought you were pressed for time and, I'm not sure what I'm wearing has to do with anything."

"Oh, come on. Like you don't know grey sweatpants are basically male lingerie as far as women are concerned."

"Wait—what?" He was so confused.

"Trust me. Google it if you don't believe me."

He held her hand as they walked along the shore. The sun was just coming up over the horizon and there was a fog in the lower lying areas of the sand dunes. The quiet of the morning and the warmth of her hand in his brought him a sense of peacefulness.

"I can see why people love coming here."

"Yeah, me too." She stared out at the sun coming up from the ocean and sighed. "It's very serene. I almost don't hate you for waking me up to the see this."

He pulled her against his side with a laugh. "Glad to hear it. What are your plans today?"

"I'm guessing breakfast with everyone, then we'll all head to the beach. Maybe play some volleyball. Yvette and I will drink and lie around. I'll try to read a book but will probably end up watching all the people that are hooking up try to pretend that they're not. You should come." She cackled. "You'd fit right in. Bring your sister. Maybe someone new is coming today, and we can try to pair her off, too."

"She's not getting paired off with anyone for a while," he growled. "Besides, she mentioned spending the day with friends of hers that are also staying on the island." Evan leaned closer to whisper in her ear, "That means the house will be empty. You won't have to be quiet."

She'd been so noisy last night that he'd had to cover her mouth with his hand—although he'd come to realize that she liked that, so he wasn't sure if she was purposefully being loud so he would. Either way, she quickly came after that—screaming into his hand as he pounded her from behind.

It'd been fucking hot, and it hadn't taken him long to finish deep inside her while her cunt was still milking him. That was quickly becoming his favorite way to come. Although, in her mouth and on her face was a close second.

"But I like it when you have to muffle me," she purred.

Goddammit, now his cock was stirring.

"There are other ways I can do that, socialite. My hands around your throat or my dick rammed in your mouth, just to name a few."

Hope glanced down at his crotch and must have noticed the outline of his growing cock, because she sighed. "Listen. I can't take your grey sweatpants *and* dirty talk this early in the morning and not be in bed doing something about it. So, behave."

"Is that a yes for this afternoon, then?"

"Come over and hang out with me on the beach—maybe play some volleyball, and we'll see if we can sneak away without it being too obvious."

"You don't think your brother will mind me being there?"

"No. You both were on your best behavior last night, so as long as you two can keep up the civility, it should be fine."

"I'll behave if he will."

"He's so wrapped up in Whitney, he might not even notice you're there."

It was odd to not be triggered by that. Evan had even found himself happy for his former friend when Steven had his arms wrapped around Whitney the entire night. The woman seemed to calm him.

Kind of like how Hope made him feel.

Based on her reaction last night, he knew he was going to have to ease her into thinking of their relationship as anything more than sex. He probably ought to begin by explaining the misunderstanding about Steven and Olivia, but not yet.

That would entail him having to apologize to his former nemesis and formally make amends. His pride would prefer that happen gradually. Besides, he knew one of Hope's kinks was sneaking around.

It was one of his, too, if he were being honest. The taboo aspect of their relationship was exciting. He could wait a little longer before wanting more. Besides, it'd give him more time to win her over.

It was funny; he'd began this affair wanting her to fall in love with him for revenge, now he wanted her to fall in love with him, so she returned the sentiment.

Because there was no way he could deny it anymore—he was in love with Hope Ericson.

Chapter Thirty-Six

Hope

Walking up to Zoe's, she noticed movement on the deck.

She turned to Evan and said softly, "I think I can make it from here."

He kissed her temple. "I'll see you later."

As she got closer to the house, she realized it was Yvette and James on a lounger, wrapped up in a blanket, watching the sunrise. Yvette sat between his legs, so her back was to his front, and he had his arms wrapped around her. They were both smiling like fools while a sunbeam bathed their faces in light.

"Good morning," Hope murmured to announce her presence as she walked up the deck steps. She'd almost hated to intrude on their moment. "I hope you guys didn't sleep out here. That'd kind of defeat the purpose of staying at Zoe's."

"No, we just wanted to watch the sunrise," her friend said dreamily.

Hope did an internal fist pump. *Yes! Mr. Wonderful, for the win. There's no way Yvette wouldn't want to move now.*

"It is beautiful," Hope said as she walked toward the door. "I think it's going to be a great day—that I will enjoy later because I'm going to back to bed. Enjoy your sunrise, morning people. You freaks."

"Night," the two called in unison.

Just as she suspected, the bed was still made. Yvette obviously hadn't slept there last night.

Hope peeled back the covers, kicked off her shoes, and stripped down to her bra and panties, then lay down. The bedding smelled fresh, and the mattress was comfortable, so after hardly getting any sleep last night, she was off to dreamland in record time.

****

Evan

"Are you sure you don't want to come with me?" Olivia asked for the fifth time as she stood in the entryway with her keys in hand and her arm wrapped through a picnic basket handle.

"Positive. I'm going to go play volleyball and hang out at Steven's."

"With Hope."

"And everyone else."

"But you're not going to spend time with everyone else. You're going to spend time with Hope."

"It doesn't matter who I'm spending time with, it's not going to be you and your friends."

"I'd feel bad about leaving you after you came all the way here, except I suspect your motives for accepting my invitation might not have been solely to spend time with me."

"Wh-at?" Evan asked in a voice two octaves higher than normal. "Now you're just talking crazy."

His sister looked at him with pursed lips. "Mm-hmm."

"Okay, I'll admit—knowing she wasn't far might have played a factor. But I'm glad we've been able to spend time together and talk. It's been too long."

"I agree, and I'm glad I got to meet Hope outside of the hospital." She opened the door. "Make sure you clean up the breakfast dishes like you promised before you go."

He offered a half-hearted salute. "Yes, ma'am."

"I mean it, Evan. I'm not your maid. If I come back to a mess, I'm going to be pissed."

"Give me a little credit, would you? I do manage not to live in filth in between my housekeeper's visits."

"Okay," she said reluctantly. "Have fun." She closed the door but just before shutting it, opened it back an inch to yell, "Don't get in a fight with Steven! And make sure you clean the kitchen!"

He shook his head and chuckled. She was going to be a great mom.

Chapter Thirty-Seven

Hope

She and Evan were on opposing volleyball teams, which worked out well, since it was easier for her to ogle him from the other side of the net.

His broad chest and six-pack were impressive—especially when he'd jump and spike the ball. Fortunately, four years of volleyball in high school and club volleyball in college made her a formidable opponent.

It was fortuitous that Steven had opted not to play before Evan even showed up, saying he and Whitney needed to go to the market for food supplies.

Dakota, who had made lunch for the group yesterday with Aiden, wrinkled her brows at his comment, but said nothing. Hope got the feeling that Steve and Whitney were going through some growing pains in their relationship. She hoped things worked out. She'd never seen her brother happier.

Evan's team beat hers—two games to one, and while it pained her to give up and not demand a best of five series, she agreed with everyone else that it was too hot.

"Steve's not staying inside because of me, is he?" Evan asked when the two were alone, pulling water bottles from the ice chest.

"No. He and Whitney went food shopping and were going to grab lunch while they're out." She said with a laugh,

"I think he's regretting inviting all these people instead of spending the weekend here alone with her."

He stared at her for a second. "I can understand that. Wanting her all to himself."

She cocked an eyebrow at him. "I'm not above punching you in front of all these people."

He let out a defensive laugh. "What? Why? What did I do?"

"You're trying to be charming. How many times have I told you to knock it off?"

"You know, someday you might not mind so much."

How could she tell him she already loved it—and that's why they needed to cool things off between them?

She spun on the balls of her feet and called, "Not likely," over her shoulder.

****

Evan

They kept up the facade that they weren't hooking up, along with Aiden and Dakota. Yvette and James didn't stop touching each other any time one of them was within reach of the other—which was basically the whole time.

They'd been separated during volleyball, which proved to be to Evan's advantage because James was a good player, while Yvette... not so much.

Zoe and Dakota cheered from their beach chairs on the sidelines, drinking the sangrias Zoe poured them from a pitcher she'd brought down from her house.

Zach, Aiden, Yvette, and Hope, versus him, James, Rolando, and Barbie meant the teams weren't very well-matched. Barbie was only good for jumping up and down—which Evan didn't necessarily mind watching, but that was about it. He did have to give props to Hope. She turned out to be the other team's secret weapon and had been underestimated when it came to picking teams. Still, he wasn't surprised when his team won and loved having the bragging rights.

Hope was not a gracious loser, to say the least, which only made talking about it all day that much sweeter.

"Nobody cares about your stupid win," she grumbled when he and James, who seemed to enjoy reveling in the victory and rubbing it in as much as Evan did, were reliving some of their stellar plays.

In the grand scheme of greatest volleyball plays of all time, they weren't really that stellar. But that didn't stop them from talking about them like they were whenever Hope was within earshot.

That was until he whispered in her ear, "Wanna take the dogs for a walk?" and she replied, "Nope. I need to practice."

That brought the smack talk to a halt, fast.

They did sneak away later, after her ego had recovered.

And he finger fucked her to an orgasm with her brother not ten feet away while they watched fireworks. Her gasps intermingled with everyone else's—only hers weren't from the pyrotechnics.

Evan knew he was playing with fire, especially since Steve scowled the minute he stepped onto the beach and saw Evan, but the opportunity had been too hard to resist.

With a grin, he pulled his hand away from her pussy and licked his ring finger.

"You are the devil," she whispered while she tried to hide her own smile.

"Sinning's never been so much fun, angel."

When he woke up with her in his arms for the second day in a row, he thought, *I could get used to this*.

Minus the walk of shame along the beach, of course. Although he actually enjoyed that. The second day she was grumpier than the first at being woken up at first light, but then again admitted to enjoying seeing the sunrise.

"Careful, socialite. We might make a morning person out of you yet."

"Considering I'm going right back to bed the minute I walk in the door, that's doubtful," she drawled.

He would have much rather she'd just stayed in his bed, but… someday.

Baby steps.

CHAPTER THIRTY-EIGHT

Hope

She and Yvette were getting ready to leave for their first bed-and-breakfast. Evan had been called back to the hospital shortly after he walked her to Zoe's, and everyone else, other than her brother and Whitney, had left.

Except James.

He was currently standing at the open driver's side door of his Porsche Taycan, making out with Hope's BFF.

When he finally drove off, Yvette came back inside with a tear-stained face.

Hope hugged her around her shoulders. "You okay?"

"Geography is a stupid whore."

"You know, there's an easy fix for that."

Her friend glared at her through watery eyes. "Your diabolical plan is coming together."

She unapologetically clapped her hands in front of her. "Yay! Let's go look at some bed-and-breakfasts!"

They visited two and stayed at three different ones. None were anything either woman wanted to invest their time, energy, or money in.

"We'll keep looking," Hope told Yvette on the drive back to Boston.

"When? I leave tomorrow morning."

"You'll just have to come back. I'm sure James won't object to that. Speaking of... are you two still having dinner tonight?"

"Last time I heard from him, that was the plan. What about you? Are you seeing Evan tonight?"

"I don't think so. He's probably working."

"Probably? You don't know for sure?"

"He's been working a lot, and I haven't been very good about returning his texts."

"Why?"

"Things are getting a little too serious. I need to slow things down."

"Serious is a bad thing? At our age?"

Hope sighed. "Yes. This was never supposed to be anything more than sex."

It'd been hard not texting him back—as a matter-of-fact, it'd sucked, but it was what she needed to do.

"Um, I'm sure you know what you're doing, but... I don't understand why you wouldn't want things to get serious. You two obviously like each other—a lot, and the sex is the best you've ever had—you said so yourself."

"Because Steve hates him."

"He seemed fine this weekend."

"He's a player."

"You said you have an agreement that you're monogamous. Do you think he's seeing other people?"

"No."

"Then I fail to see…"

"It's just a bad idea, okay?" she exclaimed in a raised voice. "It would never work."

Yvette shrugged, like she wasn't bothered. "I think you're wrong and you're just scared. But what do I know? I've only been your best friend for sixteen years."

Hope ignored her BFF's comments and said brightly, "So, where are you and James going for dinner? Do you know?"

****

Evan

He hadn't heard from Hope since he left the Cape on Sunday. He hadn't thought much about it, since he knew she and Yvette were going to visit bed-and-breakfasts and he'd been busy working. But by the time Friday rolled around without any word from her, he had to wonder what was going on. Last he knew, Yvette was leaving Thursday morning and Hope was planning on going back to work Thursday afternoon. She should have found time to reply now.

His shift ended at ten in the morning, but instead of heading toward the exit doors after he grabbed a shower and changed out of his scrubs, he went in the other direction toward Hope's office. He was relieved to see from the end of the hall that her door was open.

"Knock, knock," he said when he stood in the doorway.

She looked up from her computer and gave him a polite smile.

"Hey. What are you up to?"

"Just headed home. Thought I'd stop and see if you wanted to grab dinner tonight."

"Why?"

Her question and the harsh tone with which she delivered it took him aback. "Because I haven't seen you since Sunday."

"I mean, we can get together later, but I think dinner would be a bad idea."

It was his turn to ask, "Why?"

"Things are getting too… familiar between us. We need to go back to following the rules. We created them for a reason. I think until we can do that, we should limit how much time we see each other."

He didn't like her glib attitude. After the weekend they'd just had, he'd been expecting her to be as happy to see him as he was her, not aloof and distant and talking about her goddamn rules. Perhaps she needed a reminder about who the fuck she was talking to.

"Yeah, about those rules…" He walked further into her office, closed the door behind him, then went to stand next to her. Tugging her head back by her hair so she was forced to look at him, he continued in a low tone, "We need to have a chat about them—over dinner. Tonight. Then I'm going to fuck you hard and come on your tits, and you're going to thank me for doing so by cleaning my cock with your mouth. Then we're going to talk some more—maybe even cuddle."

He released her hair, half-expecting another sock to the stomach. Instead, she just stared up at him and said nothing.

Evan rested his hand on the back of her chair and leaned closer. "I'll pick you up at six. Wear something you don't mind being ripped off you later."

She opened her mouth, as if to respond, but then closed it again. He stood tall and walked out of her office without another word.

Limit our time together, my ass.

Chapter Thirty-Nine

Hope

She watched him walk out the door, still at a loss for words.

What the hell just happened? And why were her nipples stiff?

He must have pheromones she was attracted to. That was the only explanation she could come up with as to why, whenever she was around him, she didn't care about her rules.

There's no sense arguing with him, she told herself when she left work on time, so she was home and ready by six. He'd just pound on the door until she let him in.

I could not be home when he got here...

That was a possibility.

So why, when she got home from work, did she find herself looking for a dress to wear that she didn't care if it got ruined, instead of leaving?

And why did her heart flutter and her stomach do flips when the doorbell rang precisely at one minute before six?

****

Evan

Her dress was in tatters on his living room floor, just like he'd promised. And her tits were covered in his cum and her mouth was glistening from where she'd cleaned his cock—also as promised.

Now he was going to lick her pussy and make her come again. That had been more of an implied guarantee, but one she should have counted on.

He lay on the floor, his body perpendicular to the sofa and his head resting on a throw pillow, and he tapped his chin.

"Get on."

"Excuse me?"

"You heard me. Sit your delicious cunt on my mouth. Right. Now."

She stared at him for half a second before moving into position on his face with a sigh—like having her pussy eaten was such a burden.

Their evening had started out awkward, as he expected after her attempt to ghost him, but by the time they'd ordered dinner, they were talking and teasing like nothing had changed.

When they walked through his front door and he tore her bodice down the center without so much as a warning, things were back to normal.

He'd smiled when he held her against the wall by her throat while he fondled her pussy and found her completely drenched. *That's my girl.*

She came with a vengeance within minutes. But then again, so had he. After bending her over the couch and pounding her pussy, he spun her around and pushed her to her knees to come on her tits. She cleaned him off without even being told to.

And now she was sitting on his face with her hands gripping the couch for support as he tongued her tight hole and rubbed her little nub with his fingers.

She ground on his face and moaned loudly, so he moved his tongue and fingers faster.

Whimpering, "Yes," over and over, her thighs tightened around his head and then he felt his face flood with her delicious juices as she lurched forward and let out a long moan of, "Oh my god, yessssss!"

He didn't stop until she stilled his face between her hands.

"The devil," she whispered when she looked down at his glistening face then swung her leg off him.

He sat up and pulled her into his lap before she could go anywhere.

"Come on, angel. It's cuddle and pillow talk time."

Chapter Forty

Hope

Steven had all but moved in with Whitney. He was never at the condo, and the last time she saw Lola was when they were at the Cape.

That was probably for the best, so he wasn't keeping track of her coming and going. Hope was at Evan's a lot more than she cared to admit for someone who was supposed to be cooling things off.

He made it so hard, though. Damn him and his chiseled jaw, blue eyes, and dirty mouth.

And now he was being *nice* to her, doing things like bringing her dinner when she worked late in the lab, or sending her good morning texts on the nights she didn't sleep over because he was working. So, that made it incredibly easy to ignore the rules—which was exactly what he told her they were going to do last Friday when they had dinner and filthy sex.

She hadn't agreed in so many words, but she didn't put up much of a fight, other than stipulate that their affair had to remain a secret. Her brother no longer snarled when he said Evan's name, but he made it clear he still wasn't the man's biggest fan. And Hope pretended like it made no difference to her one way or another.

Evan had respected that. She suspected that he worried if it came down to choosing him or her brother, she'd choose her brother.

Which she would.

Probably.

Then Steven showed up at the condo ridiculously early the following Saturday morning and everything changed.

Chapter Forty-One

Hope

She felt her arm being nudged. "Hey, little sister. Wake up."

Her first instinct was to swear at the intruder and pull the covers over her head, but before she did, her brain caught up with her.

Steven was in her room, waking her up. He never did that.

"What happened? Is everything okay?" she asked as she sat up with a jolt.

He pressed on her shoulder as if trying to assure her. "Everything's fine. I just need to talk to you. I have some news."

She held her breath, and he sat down on the edge of the bed with a smile and said, "Relax, it's good news. I wanted you to be one of the first to know."

Her eyebrows lifted, and she nodded her head, encouraging him to continue.

"You're going to be an aunt."

She sat there, trying to process what he was telling her. She distinctly remembered Ava confiding in her that Travis had gotten a vasectomy after their third child was born, and Grace was the one who had encouraged Hope to get an implant after she'd gotten one.

That meant…

Her eyes went wide as a big smile spread across her face and she squealed, "Is Whitney pregnant? Are you guys having a baby?"

Steven was half-laughing, half-crying when he spit out, "Yes!"

She wrapped her arms around his shoulders and squeezed. Since she still hadn't brushed her teeth, she was careful to turn her head away from him when she gushed, "I am so happy for you. Congratulations!"

"Okay, now the bad news."

Hope pulled away and covered her mouth with her hand. "How could there possibly be bad news? If you think you moving out is bad news, I hate to break it to you, but you pretty much already have."

"You can't tell anybody."

Her shoulders slumped, and she pulled her hand away—morning breath be damned. "Oh, man. You know I'm the worst at keeping secrets. Why would you put that pressure on me?"

Steve lifted her wrist and put her hand back to her mouth with a smirk.

"It's not that hard; you just don't bring it up. Nobody else is going to bring it up because… why would they?"

"Yeah, but then Mom's going to say something like, "How's Steven and his girlfriend doing? And I'm going to be like, 'Oh, they're great. Just out crib shopping.' See? I'm going to cave."

"You won't cave. I have faith in you."

"Misguided faith," she grumbled.

"Would you rather I hadn't told you?"

"Well, no. I'd have been hurt if you hadn't."

"Exactly. Don't make me regret telling you."

"When did you find out?"

"Last night. Whitney's still in shock. We're going to go to the Cape and get away for the night. Her friend Gwen is going with us to help her process."

"Oh no. Is she not happy?"

"Probably not as much as I am right now. This was unexpected and not in her 'life plan.' But, she'll come around."

"You're right—she will. I can imagine if you guys weren't trying, this is quite a surprise."

"To say the least."

"So, I'm assuming you're taking me to breakfast, since you woke me up at this ungodly hour."

"I wish I could, but we're leaving for the Cape at eight. Do you wanna come?"

"No, I was planning on working in the lab all weekend." Evan was scheduled in the ER both Saturday and Sunday, so Hope thought she'd go in and work while he was. And, of course, go back to his place when he was finished.

Steve stood up. "Let's have dinner when I get back. I feel like we never see each other, and we live in the same condo."

She wrinkled her nose. "Mmm, I guess on paper, but let's be real. You live at Whitney's. Hell, *your dog* lives at Whitney's. I haven't seen Lola since the Fourth."

"I know. Do you hate me for talking you into moving to Boston and then not being here for you?"

"Not at all. I love it here, and I'm happy you're happy."

"It's probably a good thing you moved during the summer; you might be singing a different tune come January when you're digging your car out."

"I'm not digging my car out. I paid for covered parking here and the hospital gave me a premium spot in the parking garage."

"Yeah, I've seen where you park. Right between Liam McDonnell and Parker."

"To be honest, I wasn't expecting *that* good of a spot when I asked Parker for a reserved space a few weeks ago. Although I didn't mind—I can't imagine either the hospital CEO or chief of staff dinging my car."

"I'm surprised their cars aren't covered in dust. They never leave."

"That makes me sad."

Steve lifted his shoulders. "They love their jobs."

"That's what makes me sad. They love their jobs at the detriment of loving anyone else."

"I don't think either would be opposed to finding a girlfriend. But it's not exactly like they can date someone from the hospital staff, so…"

"They need to get out more."

He stood and walked toward the door. "I agree. They're both going to the fundraiser for the animal rescue Whitney and Dakota are a part of, so there's that." He had a sly smile when he turned around. "Aiden's going too—and he never goes to anything anymore. I was shocked when he came to the Cape."

"He seems like a good guy. Grumpy, but a good guy."

"He wasn't always that way. His ex-wife burned him bad."

"That sucks."

"Yeah..."

They were quiet for an awkward beat, then Hope gave him a big smile. "Congratulation, *Dad*."

"Now I'm going to have two people calling me daddy."

She tossed a pillow at him. "Ew! I did not need to know that!"

He dodged the pillow easily with a laugh. "I'm just kidding. Whitney would never call me that."

"No, I can't see her using that term with you."

"Yeah, it'd be like you using it."

Did sir count? She gave a nervous laugh. "Gosh, could you imagine?"

"No." He tapped her doorframe. "I'll call you tomorrow when I get back. Love you."

"Love you, too!"

She flopped onto her back. Steven was going to have a baby. If he disowned her now, she'd lose out on being a part of his baby's life.

It didn't matter—it wasn't going to happen. Evan Lacroix was just a temporary, secret fling.

*

Three days later, Parker pulled her from her office. "You need to take Steven home. Whitney lost the baby."

Chapter Forty-Two

Evan

He knew when he saw Whitney being wheeled down the hall in the ER that it wasn't going to be good news.

Forty-five minutes later, he heard her yelling, "Go! Leave!" and an ashen Steven stumbled from her room.

Evan texted Hope that she needed to come down to the ER right away.

She replied: **Parker just told me. I'm on my way**.

He saw her a few minutes later hugging her brother. When he looked again, they were both gone.

Hope kept him updated on the situation. Evan didn't envy the man—he lost his baby and his girlfriend in one day.

Evan couldn't even imagine.

He made a special trip to see his sister when he got off work and gave her a big hug.

"What was that for?" she asked with a laugh as they broke apart.

"Steven's girlfriend, Whitney, lost her baby today."

Tears formed in his sister's eyes, and she brought her hand to her mouth. "Oh, no. I didn't even know she was pregnant. That's awful."

She sat down and bawled for twenty minutes straight.

"Why would you tell a pregnant woman that?" she sobbed.

Oh fuck.

"I don't know! I thought, 'you're going to find out eventually' and then you'd be mad at me for not telling you!"

"And I would have been!" She dabbed her eyes and sob-laughed.

"So basically you're telling me there's no way I could've won in this situation."

"Basically."

"Good to know. Can I look forward to more of this for the next four months?"

"Yep."

He pulled her in to hug her around her shoulders and kiss her forehead.

"I'll take it."

"Tell Hope I'm so sorry and that I'm thinking of Steven and Whitney. They must be devastated."

"Yeah. It wasn't pretty. She kicked him out of her room. Hope said she broke up with him."

"Oh, god—poor guy. Grief is a funny thing. Hopefully, she'll be able to gain some perspective and they'll patch things up."

Evan ended up covering several of Steve's shifts that week. He knew Hope was going to be with her brother as soon as she left work, so he wouldn't be seeing her anyway. And maybe doing so would buy him some goodwill from Steven in the process.

On Friday, he stopped in to see Hope in her office. She looked gorgeous, as usual. As much as he'd love to fuck her on her desk, he'd just worked sixteen hours for the third day that week and was tired.

"You look like hell," she said when she looked up from her computer screen and saw him standing in the doorway.

He walked in and sunk down into the chair opposite her. Big mistake. He might not be able to get back up.

"I feel like hell. How's Steve?"

"He rock bottomed Wednesday and is slowly digging his way out. He's excited to see Whitney at the ARF Gala tonight. But I'm worried that's not going to go the way he hopes."

"The gala is tonight? I'm guessing you're going?"

"Parker invited me to be part of his table, but I'd already committed to Steven's. Now, I'm glad I stuck with going with my brother."

"What are you wearing?" he asked with a grin.

"The standard little black dress."

God, he missed her.

"I'll bet you're going to look hot. I'd pay good money to see that. And take it off you afterward."

The corner of her mouth turned up. "I think Parker has an extra ticket…"

Evan suddenly found himself awake enough to seek out his boss.

****

Hope

Steven's head was on a swivel when they walked into the ballroom. A pretty girl with blue hair offered to show them to their seats. Just as Steven replied, "Sure," Hope saw Evan in a black suit and purple tie. It was hard to remain unaffected when all she wanted to do was fan herself.

Oh. My. God. He is so hot.

She took a play right out of her mother's handbook and put her hand on Steven's shoulder. "Excuse me. I see some people I need to say hello to. I'll catch up with you."

Evan caught her eye as she made her way to the bar, and with the same gesture she'd just used on her brother, excused himself from the group he was talking to.

"Fancy meeting you here," she said quietly when he stood next to her while they waited to get the bartender's attention. The guy could take his time.

"You look fucking amazing. I can't wait to see this dress on my floor later."

"That's rather presumptuous of you, Dr. Lacroix," she teased while staring straight ahead.

"Perhaps. But I like my odds."

Hope wasn't going to bet against him.

"I'm here with my brother."

"I know. But you're going home with me."

"I don't think I am. Maybe I can get away tomorrow."

"I work tomorrow—which is why you need to be in my bed tonight. I miss you."

The bartender finally appeared, and Hope said, "White wine, please," with her polite smile while Evan ordered a bourbon and soda on the rocks.

"I miss you, too," she said quietly. "But now more than ever, we need to keep this a secret."

"I get it. You don't want to upset your brother any more than he already is."

The wine was delivered, and she grasped it in both hands when she turned to face him. "Thank you." Then she winked. "Maybe we could find a supply closet somewhere around here."

Evan took a swig of his drink. "I'm on it. I'll text you when I find one."

She got a text thirty minutes later.

****

Evan

He sat at his table watching—Hope, because, well, he was a caveman, and also the staff as they walked around because he was formulating a plan. He observed the hallways they came in and out of and excused himself to investigate further.

Behind the stage, there was an open area with empty dog crates, blankets, and dog dishes. There was a large storage room in the middle of the back wall, where the girl with the blue streaks in her hair was leaning against a table, texting.

But in a dark corner of the room, almost hidden by some heavy stage curtains, there was a janitor's closet.

He sent Hope a text: **It's not a supply closet, more like a janitor one. But it has a lock, and it's secluded in a hidden corner.**

Hope: Where?

Evan: Backstage.

Hope: I'll be right there on one condition.

Evan: Oh, you're specifying conditions now.

Hope: You can't mess up my makeup. I paid good money to have it done professionally.

She had looked amazing; he'd give her that.

Evan: I'll do my best. But when we get back to my place tonight, I'm smearing your lipstick all over my cock.

Hope: We'll see. I haven't said I would go home with you.

Evan: You will.

Minutes later, she appeared in the entry. Evan grabbed her hand, put a finger to his lips and pointed to the open storeroom, then pulled her through the shadows along the edge of the wall until they reached their destination.

She followed him inside the tiny room and closed the door behind her. Evan crowded her against it as he reached down to turn the lock on the handle, then refused to move from her space.

"I hope you didn't wear any panties," he growled in her ear while he cupped her breast, fighting the urge to kiss her mouth that was inches from his.

"I guess you'll just have to find out for yourself."

Inching her dress up her thighs, he let his hand wander under the hem. She was wearing thigh highs and nothing else under the fabric.

"You dirty little slut." He chuckled as he dipped his hand between her seam. "You were hoping to get fucked tonight, weren't you?"

She simply nodded while he plunged a finger inside her, then spread her wetness around her folds. Repeating the motion until she gasped.

Rubbing her clit in circles, he chastised, "You need to be quiet, socialite."

"I—uh. Oh."

Evan covered her mouth with one hand and with the other, played her pussy like it was an instrument and he was the maestro. Not two minutes later, she was coming on his fingers.

"Such a naughty girl. That's why you like these secret trysts."

"Don't act like you don't love them too," she sassed as she rubbed his hard cock over his suit pants.

"I wouldn't dream of it."

He positioned himself behind her and faced her away from the door. Pressing on her back so she was bent over, she grabbed hold of a shelf that held cleaning supplies. He pulled her dress even high above her waist and stared at her luscious ass as he freed his cock from his pants. Grabbing her hips, he thrust deep inside her wet heat.

"Fuuuuck," he grunted through gritted teeth. "Your pussy feels so good."

Thankfully, the shelves were anchored securely to the wall and only rattled a little as he fucked her hard and fast.

He came inside her and held himself there with his head on her back until his breathing evened out.

Finally, he pulled out and tucked himself back in his pants. "Hope Ericson. You are a naughty slut and I love yo—er, it."

She gave him the side eye as she swiped between her legs with a paper towel she'd pulled from the shelf she'd just been holding on to for dear life.

"Well, I love being a naughty slut with you."

There was no acknowledgment of his faux pas, and she shimmied her dress back down her hips.

"How's my hair?"

"Not a one out of place."

He opened the door and peeked out to see if the coast was clear. When he was satisfied they were safe, he stepped outside and almost ran right into Parker, who seemed to be looking for the exit by the curtains.

Aw, shit.

Evan quickly pushed the door closed in Hope's face.

"Parker!" he said loudly, so she'd understand why he'd done that.

The chief of staff nodded at him, and Evan searched his brain for what he was going to say was the reason why he was lurking around in the backstage shadows.

This wasn't going to go well. Evan had promised he'd keep a low profile.

But instead of questioning Evan about what he was doing in the backstage area, Parker smiled nervously and pointed toward the exit by the curtains.

"Was just looking for the bathroom and got lost."

Huh. That's the excuse Evan was going to give his boss.

Before he could respond, Parker disappeared. Evan opened the closet door to find Hope with wide eyes.

"That was too close for comfort," she whispered. "Do you think he suspected?"

He shook his head slowly, trying to make sense of what just happened. "No, he seemed to want to get out of here as quickly as possible."

"I wonder what he was doing back here?"

Just then the storage room door opened, and the young woman with the blue streaks pulled on the bottom of her dress, glanced down at the bodice, and quickly buttoned two buttons that were opened.

"Not what—" He looked slyly at Hope. "Who."

"Good for Parker," she murmured as she watched the woman walk across the floor to the more popular exit with her head held high. "And good for her."

"They may be on to something... You go that way." Evan pointed to where the woman had just disappeared. "And I'll go this way," he said, pointing to the heavy curtain Parker had slipped behind.

"If anyone sees you coming from where Parker just came from, people are going to talk," she teased.

"Let 'em. Parker's a stud."

"It would throw off any suspicions about us, that's for sure."

"We better get back before people notice we're missing at the same time."

He leaned down to kiss her but stopped short when he looked at her perfectly made-up face.

"I'm kissing the fuck out of you later. Your lipstick is going to be smeared all over your face then my cock," he warned, then disappeared behind the curtain.

CHAPTER FORTY-THREE

Hope

She grabbed another glass of wine from the bar before she sat down next to her brother. James was there with a date who looked like he'd just pulled her off the pole. Zach had the matching set.

Normally she wouldn't cast judgment about that, except James had just been doting on her BFF two weeks ago. He was supposed to be Mr. Wonderful, who was the last cog in getting Yvette to move east.

So much for that. *Thanks for nothing, asshole.*

After giving James the stink eye, she bent sideways toward her brother sitting next to her. "How you holding up?"

"I'm okay. And by okay, I mean, by a thread. She took off in the opposite direction when she saw me earlier."

Hope put her hand over Steven's clenched fist on the table. "I'm sorry. This has to be hard on her, too."

"Of course, it is. But we should be grieving together."

"I know." She didn't know what else to say. She wanted to be optimistic, but not offer false hope.

"Lola hates me. She hasn't stopped moping around since Billy brought her home from Whitney's. All she does is look at me like she wants to bite me, then sigh loudly as she plops on the big bed she used to share with Ralph."

"Lola doesn't hate you. She just misses Ralph. She'll be fine."

"I hope so. I can't lose my girl *and* my dog." He looked at her with a sad smile. "At least I've got you."

She wrapped both arms around his bicep and rested her head on his shoulder. "You'll always have me."

A pit in her stomach began to form.

She needed to tell Evan they should see other people. There was no future for them. The sneaking around and the taboo aspect of what they were doing had been hot, and it'd been a lot of fun, but she needed to find someone she could bring home at the holidays, hold hands with in public, introduce to people, tell her brother about. Not meet in janitor closets just to be together at an event.

This needed to end.

Soon.

"Do you mind taking care of Lola for a while? I'm going to head to the Cape after this. Try to get my head on right. I'm not sure how long I'll be gone."

"You're leaving tonight? Do you think that's a good idea?"

"Aw, look who's channeling Francine," he teased.

"Well, I have reason to worry. It's going to be late, and you're going to be tired. Why don't you leave now?"

"Well, for three reasons. One, I sponsored this table and asked all these people to come and spend their money. I think it'd be rude to just leave in the middle of it. Definitely not Frannie approved. Two, I've had a few drinks. And, three, I'm hungry and I want to have dinner."

"Makes sense."

He sat for a second, lost in thought. "I need to do something big."

That made her nervous. She didn't want her brother humiliated in front of everyone when he made a grand gesture and Whitney turned him down. "That only works in the movies. This is not the time to risk your reputation—especially when you're not sure it will work. People are already talking."

"I know they are. There's not much I can do about that."

"Other than rise above it." They both said in unison—quoting their mother.

Steve's attention was on the area where the silent auction items were. Hope wasn't surprised to find Whitney standing among the tables, talking to guests.

A slow smile crept along her brother's face. "I know what I'm going to do," he said as he stood up.

She wanted to stop him, but he seemed so determined that she didn't say anything. Glancing around the table, she noticed his friends watching him, too. She and Aiden exchanged looks, both seemed to express, "There's nothing we can do."

Hope expected Steve to do something crazy like leap on stage and start singing "You've Lost That Lovin' Feeling." Instead, she watched as he sought out someone working the event, and they disappeared into a side room.

She looked over to where Evan sat and found him watching her. When their eyes met, he winked and smiled softly.

It made her toes curl, and she looked at her hands in her lap while pressing her lips together to hide her smile. That only made him smile wider, and she saw his chest move, as if he were laughing.

"Excuse me. I see someone I need to say hello to," she told her tablemates as she got up. There may have been an extra sway in her hips as she walked toward Parker's table—Evan's eyes were laser-focused on her.

She returned his stare, and he seemed surprised when she walked right by him and stopped in front of Parker and Liam.

"Hello, gentlemen. Don't you both look dashing tonight," she said with a hand on the backs of both their chairs.

"Hope! You look lovely, yourself." Parker smiled as he turned toward her. "How's Steven?"

She took a deep breath and sighed. "Healing."

"That's good to hear. Obviously, we miss him in the ER, but everyone's pitching in and covering for him—especially Dr. Lacroix."

She looked over at Evan as if just noticing he was there. "Dr. Lacroix, good to see you. That's very considerate of you. Thank you. I'm sure my brother appreciates it."

I appreciate it.

"I'm happy to help."

"Well, I should get back to my table. I think they're about to serve dinner. I just wanted to stop and say hello."

"Save me a dance later," Evan blurted out before she walked away.

She channeled her mother when she regally replied, "Of course."

****

Evan

As Hope walked away without another word, the chief of staff looked at Evan suspiciously—like he was wondering if Evan had lied about why he wanted the extra ticket for tonight. Fortunately, the woman from the storage closet appeared at their table and his boss seemed to forget all about Evan.

"Alexandra," he greeted her warmly. "Did you find someone to adopt Gus and Maggie?"

Gus and Maggie were the older black Labradors she'd been walking around introducing to people.

She shook her head sadly. "No, not yet."

"Don't give up hope. I'm sure someone will step up."

Evan couldn't help but notice as Parker subtly traced a finger along the woman's calf, or the way she touched his arm.

Hmm, looks like Parker might be the owner of two black labs soon. Along with a woman half his age.

Good for Parker. The woman seemed spunky enough to keep Parker on his toes.

He glanced to where Hope was sitting at her table. There was something to be said for spunky women.

Chapter Forty-Four

Hope

"I'm going to head out. Here's my credit card," Steven said, handing her the platinum piece of plastic. "Will you pay my bill for my silent auction items and take them home with you? I should win the bottle of whiskey and the fall colors trip at a bed-and-breakfast."

B and B? That got Hope's attention. "Yeah, of course."

"The total bill is going to be a lot. Like, *a lot*. I'm expecting that."

"Does this have anything to do with your 'doing something big' declaration?"

"Yep." He kissed the top of her head. "Thanks for doing this, and for taking care of Lola."

"I live at your place for free—it's the least I can do."

He said his goodbyes to the table with a sad smile. It seemed everyone—at least the people who'd spent time with Whitney and Steven at the Cape over the Fourth—understood that he was throwing in the towel, and they wished him safe travels with long faces.

Even the stripper twins picked up on the melancholy mood. James's date stroked Steven's arm over his jacket. "If you ever want to come to the club, I can get you in the VIP room with no problem. Just get my number from Jamie."

Jamie. Barf.

He was supposed to be Mr. Wonderful for her BFF, now he was turning into his brother. Except Zach was always the life of the party, so at least his antics were tolerable—maybe expected. He'd never pretended to be something he wasn't.

James on the other hand... wrapped up in a blanket at sunrise with her best friend, whispering his hopes and dreams, and talking shit about his brother's choice of date one weekend, and not two weeks later bringing his own version of Barbie to a gala. A gala he knew Hope would be at and would probably report to Yvette about his date.

It pissed her off that he was making her do his dirty work.

Not long after her brother left, Whitney appeared at their table, looking nervously at Steven's empty chair.

"Hey, everyone," she said with a shy smile. "I have Steven's auction winnings."

"You can just leave the bottle of whiskey with me," Zach said with a grin.

"*I'll* take those," Hope said as she waved his plastic in front of her. "I have his credit card."

Hope noticed Whitney take in a deep breath and muster a smile as she walked toward Steven's empty space next to her. She handed the bottle and envelope to Hope with shaky hands; Hope's heart broke for the woman.

She set the items in front of her and stood to pull Whitney in for a long hug, as she whispered, "How are you?"

Whitney pulled away and swiped at her eyes. "I've been better."

"I'm so sorry, Whit. If there's anything I can do…"

"Did Steven leave?"

Hope tried to be gentle when she replied, "Yeah. He decided to head out to the Cape straight from here."

"Oh."

Hope had a hunch. "You could deliver these yourself… He's there alone tonight."

Whitney shook her head. "I'm not sure he'd want to see me right now. Besides, I've got Ralph."

The idea that her brother wouldn't want to see Whitney made her laugh. "Trust me, he would be thrilled to see you, and I'm happy to pick up Ralph and keep him for the weekend."

Whitney wrung her hands nervously in front of her as she contemplated Hope's suggestion.

Zach said softly, "You should go, Whitney."

James agreed, "You two need to talk."

Even Aiden nodded subtly.

"Are you sure you don't mind picking up Ralph?"

Hell no, I wouldn't mind. "No. I'd love to. Lola has been moping around since she got back, so I will definitely be the hero when I bring Ralph home with me tonight."

"I can bring him by if it'd be easier."

She wasn't going to let Whitney talk herself out of going. She grabbed the woman's forearms and looked her in the eye.

"I've got it. Tell me the lock code, and I'll get him tonight. Don't think about it anymore, just go. Leave. Right now."

Hope picked up the bottle and envelope and handed them back to Whitney. "Do not go home, do not pass go, do not collect two hundred dollars. Get in your car and head to the Cape."

Whitney took a shuddered breath and said softly, "Okay, I'll do it."

Hope hugged her hopefully future-sister-in-law's shoulders, then kissed her cheek. "He's a good man."

"I know."

Whitney's acknowledgment made Hope feel better about sending her to Steven without warning him she was coming.

Instead of texting her brother, she found herself opening a message to Evan.

Hope: I can't come to your place tonight. I have to dog sit.

Evan: Need some company?

Hope: Love some.

Evan: I'm not leaving at dawn, so don't even ask.

Her first thought was, *He'll leave at dawn if I say he will.* She even pictured herself crossing her arms stubbornly in front of her chest.

Fortunately, for the sake of not having to argue, he wouldn't need to, since Steve probably wouldn't be home all weekend.

Hope: Fine, but you're going to get breakfast in the morning.

Evan: That's what delivery is for, socialite.

Hope: I have to go pick up Ralph after I leave here.

Evan: I'll go with you.

Another text immediately followed.

Evan: Don't argue.

He thinks he knows me so well, she grumbled internally. But her first instinct when she'd first read his text *had* been to argue that it wasn't necessary.

Hope: Fine. I'll pick you up at your place, then we'll go to Whitney's. It's not far from you.

Evan: It's a date.

It's not a date!

Instead of texting back, she looked up to where he was still sitting at Parker's table to find him looking at her with a stupid grin.

She narrowed her eyes at him and mouthed, "No, it's not." At the same time, her phone buzzed in her hand.

Evan: Yeah, it is.

Hope looked over at him again, and he winked, then stood up and gestured with his head toward the door.

"Good night everyone," she said with a smile as she gathered her purse. "I have to go pick up Ralph."

She stopped by the cashier table to sign the credit card receipt. She coughed when she saw the amount. Her brother wasn't joking—it was a lot. Five figures.

Hope had to admit, in terms of grand gestures—that was a pretty damn good one.

****

Evan

He thought the neighbors were going to be pounding on the condo walls with all the high-pitched yipping taking place between Ralph and Lola.

Then, they got the zoomies and were chasing each other throughout the house, sliding into walls and knocking over anything that got in their way—chairs, end tables, Hope...

Fortunately, Hope managed to keep her balance and not fall because Evan wasn't convinced the two wouldn't have trampled her without a second thought.

"Wow—is that how you act when you know you're going to see me?" he teased.

"Yes." Sarcasm dripping from her voice. "Why do you think I'm always so sweaty?"

He knew his eyes were twinkling as he stalked toward her. "I thought it was because of what I did to make you sweaty."

"Nope, it's because I run around the house first."

He kissed her shoulder and stroked her bare arm, then nibbled on her neck. "We need to get you out of this dress."

She froze under his touch. "Hold on. Listen."

They both stood not moving, and he finally whispered, "I don't hear anything."

"Exactly." There was panic in her voice, and she headed in the direction the dogs had run off in. "They're like toddlers, you need to be nervous when you don't hear them."

They found the two conked out on the big round dog bed in the kitchen. Lola's head was on Ralph's neck, and Evan swore it looked like the two were smiling with their eyes closed.

"They're so stinking adorable." Hope took out her camera and clicked a picture. "I'm going to send this to Whitney and Steven. Hopefully, if they haven't already made up, this will inspire them."

A few minutes later, she received a notification and looked down at her screen. "Aw," she said, flashing her phone for Evan to see. It was a picture of Steven and Whitney in bed together. Steven was bare-chested and Whitney had the sheet wrapped under her arms, her bare shoulders exposed. "They made up."

Evan unzipped Hope's dress, letting it drop to the floor around her feet. "We should send them one of us like that."

He'd said it to be cheeky, but he kind of was serious. Steven needed to know about them.

Hope set her phone on the table. "Ha. Ha. You're a funny guy."

If she weren't standing in front of him in nothing but a pair of thigh highs and heels, he might have been more inclined to pursue the topic.

But when you have a naked goddess in front of you, you don't push a subject you know she doesn't want to talk about.

No, you fuck her silly.

Which was what he intended to do—all night.

Chapter Forty-Five

Hope

Over the next few weeks, Evan continued to push for them to go on dates—in public. While Hope always countered with them spending time at his place.

They had a great time together every time—and the sex continued to be adventurous and exciting, but she knew he wanted more.

Hope let out a big sigh. They needed to have a conversation—she knew she wasn't being fair by continuing to ask him to be her dirty little secret. But what choice did she have? It was either that, or end things, and she was too selfish for that.

Maybe it was time Hope stopped being so selfish and let him find someone who could give him what he wanted.

She knew he was working that night, so she sent a text and was surprised when he answered right away.

Hope: Dinner at my place tomorrow?
Evan: Does it include breakfast?
Hope: Maybe.
Evan: I'll be there.

****

Evan

"Dr. Preston! What brings you into the ER?" Evan asked as he washed his hands at the nurse's station.

"Just thought I'd swing by and see how the new staff is working out."

"The new nurses seem to have hit the ground running, and Dr. Cruz been great. We could use three more just like her."

"I know. I'm talking to the board about another physician hire, as well as two more nurses."

"I know they'd be welcomed."

"So, I don't know if you've heard, but I'm getting an award next week…"

"I did. Person of the Year. Congratulations. That's quite an honor."

"Thanks," Parker said dismissively, like he was embarrassed by it. "I'd like to invite you to be at my table at the awards banquet."

"Me? I'm flattered, but… Why me?"

"You've been working hard picking up the slack around here, so you've made me look good. I wanted to acknowledge that."

Evan wasn't buying it.

"Don't those seats go for like five hundred dollars a plate?"

"Well, yes."

"So, basically, I'm a single guy and can afford to go rub elbows with the board."

"No, no. That's not it at all. I'm buying. I thought I'd ask Hope, too."

Ah, there it is. "So, you're thinking if I agree to go, Hope will go, too. And since she's the golden child of Boston General, you want *her* there representing you..."

"Okay, yes. The thought crossed my mind that I would like to have the woman who is going to revolutionize our prosthetics department at my table. But, I was sincere when I said I wanted to acknowledge everything you've done."

Evan looked at him with a disbelieving frown, so Parker continued, "Don't forget, I got you a seat at the ARF gala. And it wouldn't hurt your career to keep showing up to events the board is at."

Evan had confided in Parker that he and Hope were *kind of* seeing each other, and that he needed a ticket to the animal rescue event to *kind of* spend some time with her without making it obvious to her brother. He'd couched it that Steven was upset about Whitney, and they didn't want him to know about them while he was still heartbroken.

Parker had looked at him skeptically about his reason but said nothing other than making Evan give him his word that the two would be discreet around the hospital, and there would be no hanky-panky on the premises. Evan may have crossed his fingers when he pledged that last part.

"You did, and I appreciate that. And you're right—it wouldn't hurt to be seen at something like that. I would be honored to go, but I don't expect you to buy my ticket. I'm happy to pay my way—on two conditions."

Parker raised his eyebrows, as if prompting him to continue.

"One, you're the one to ask Hope, not me. It would mean a lot coming from you."

"No problem. What's the second condition?"

"You tell me what's going on with you and the girl from the gala."

Chapter Forty-Six

Hope

She waited at the elevator bank, wondering what Parker wanted to see her about. Armstrong Labs had delivered her invention, and the prosthetics department was up and running with her technology producing even better results than she could have imagined. She never ceased to not cry every time they fitted a patient, and she saw the look on their face.

He better not be calling me in to complain about the pro bono work.

That had been a stipulation in her contract—up to ten percent of her patients would be the under/uninsured with little to no cost to them. And the hospital would accept VA payments as payment in full for veterans.

The *ding*! of the elevator arriving brought her back to the present.

"Five please," she said to the unlucky person stuck next to the panel of numbers taking floor requests.

"You're Hope Ericson, aren't you?" a deep voice beside her asked.

She got that a lot. The next question was always followed by, "Steven's sister?" Her brother was a popular doctor around Boston General, and she was proud to be associated with him.

"I am," she said with a smile.

Instead of the little sister question though, he asked, "Do you know if Evan's planning on playing hockey again this fall?"

"I'm sorry—Evan?"

He looked at her like she was a moron. "Evan Lacroix? You're dating him, aren't you?"

She felt the color drain from her face.

"No?"

"Oh, I didn't realize you guys broke up. I'm sorry."

The elevator had stopped on the fifth floor, otherwise she would have told the man they never were dating and there was nothing to be sorry about. Instead, she stumbled out of the car, not having said anything more.

This was a disaster. How did this get out? She took a deep breath. She thought they'd been so sly about hiding their affair. Evan had sworn they could trust Olivia. That just left… *James.*

After her meeting with Parker, she was going to find him and give him a piece of her mind. She was already pissed at him about Yvette—now he was really going to get it. And if word had gotten back to Steven… well, she didn't know what she'd do. But it would be diabolical.

At least in her daydreams.

She walked into Parker's office and Helen, his assistant, waved her through. "He's expecting you."

Still, she knocked on his open door to get his attention.

He stood with a cheerful smile. "Hope! Come in!"

"You wanted to see me?"

"Yes, thanks for coming down. Please, have a seat."

Once they were both seated, he spoke.

"You may have heard I'm receiving an award…"

"Person of the Year. Congratulations."

"I personally think it's just a way for the hospital network to raise more money, and they know people in Boston have deep pockets."

"Don't minimize your achievement, Parker. It's a big deal. You should be proud. I know I am honored to be working for you."

His face softened at her compliment. "Thank you, Hope. I'm hoping you will be my guest at the dinner next week and sit at my table. I've already asked Evan, and I was planning on talking to Steven when he comes in for his shift later."

Oh fuck. The rumor had gotten to Parker?

She decided not to address it. That's what her mother would do.

"I would be honored. Let me know where to send my check."

"That's not necessary. It's on me."

"Nonsense. You're the man being honored. You shouldn't have to pay for my seat. Besides," she winked, "I make a lot of money. I need the tax write-off."

She left Parker's office on a mission to find James Rudolf and give his gossipy ass what for.

Except, wouldn't you know it, it was his day off. She felt her bravado deflate like a balloon.

No! shouted her inner voice. *This is bullshit! I should go pound on the front door of his house!*

Paging the crazy lady in the Prada suit.

Her mother always taught her to think of how the headline would read if she got arrested. She'd done it because in San Diego it would have read: *Federal Judge's Daughter....* Her poor sister Grace had lived through that.

Now, it would read: *Boston General Employee...*

Okay, so she wouldn't go to James's house. But he was going to get an earful tomorrow.

For now, she needed to do damage control. Beginning tonight.

****

Evan

"We need to see other people."

He choked on his drink at her words. Setting his glass down and wiping his mouth, he looked at her from across the dining room table. "Um... Why?"

"People at the hospital are talking. They know we're dating. I had a guy in the elevator ask me if I knew if you were planning on playing hockey this year. He thought I would know since we. Are. Dating."

Oh yeah—he needed to sign up for the hospital's league team.

It was time for this bullshit to end.

"Hope, honey, we *are* dating."

"No, we're *not*."

He switched chairs to the one next to hers and pulled her into his lap.

"I have to tell you something. You know this rift between your brother and me? Yes, I'm the reason for it, but it's not because I'm jealous of him or upset that he got the ER director job over me. I thought he was the father of Olivia's baby and that he didn't want anything to do with Olivia or her child."

She pulled away to look at his face. "You thought my brother got your sister pregnant? And then ghosted her? *My* brother? The guy who was devastated when Whitney lost their baby?"

"Yes," he said quietly.

She got up and paced in front of him. "Well, that explains why you're screwing me."

"It's not like that, Hope."

She raised an eyebrow at him. "No? So, the first time..."

"It's not like that *anymore*. I found out I was wrong when I stayed with Olivia over the Fourth."

She cleared their plates, obviously lost in thought. Evan sat stark still, waiting for her to say something.

Finally, she swung around from where she stood at the sink. "So, you think just because you don't hate my brother anymore, that everything's okay? Nothing's changed, Evan—other than your perspective. Steven still can't stand you and would disown me if he knew I was with you."

"You're being a little dramatic—don't you think? You honestly think your brother would disown you if he found out we were dating?"

"I don't know, but I'm not willing to risk it. He and Whitney are going to be having babies soon, and I'm going to be a part of his children's lives."

"What about your babies, Hope? Our babies? The ones we could have together."

Her eyes bugged out. "Are you out of your mind? We were a fling, Evan. Temporary. Something to pass the time until something better came along."

Her words were like a knife to the gut.

"I know we started out that way, but that's not how it is now, and you know it."

Hope rubbed her forehead and sighed. "Look, I think we need to see other people and squash these rumors."

"I don't want to see other people."

"We can still see each other—secretly. But this can't ever be anything more than a clandestine affair, Evan. My brother can never know about us."

He sat in his chair, digesting her words. He knew he needed to fix this, he just didn't know how. Finally, he stood up and murmured, "I'm going to go."

"Okay, yeah. That's probably for the best."

She walked him to the door. "Let's take some time apart. Go on a few dates with other people, and check in with each other in a couple of weeks."

That wasn't going to work.

Still, he found himself saying, "Yeah, okay."

He flinched when she stood on her tiptoes and tried to kiss his cheek. "Take care. We'll talk soon."

He felt like a zombie as he walked to his car. *So this is what it feels like to have a broken heart.*

****

Hope

She closed the door behind him and proceeded to the powder room, where she promptly threw up her dinner.

Chapter Forty-Seven

Hope

Now why was she being summoned to Parker's office?

Once again, Helen waved her through. She lifted her knuckle to knock, then noticed Evan sitting on Parker's tan leather couch talking with Parker, who was seated in a matching tufted armchair.

After crying herself to sleep, it was jarring to see him again so soon. Thank goodness she'd put tea bags on her eyes that morning before getting ready for work.

"Is this a bad time?"

"Hope! No, we were just waiting for you."

After a brief pause, she willed her feet toward the sitting area, trying to appear blasé.

"What's going on?" she asked as she sat in the chair next to Parker, opposite Evan.

Parker gestured to the drinks on a tray on the table, and Hope shook her head.

"I need a favor." She appreciated that Parker didn't beat around the bush.

"Okay?" she replied. She felt her mouth go dry as she ran through the possible scenarios of favors that would involve her and Evan. Changing her mind about that drink after all, she leaned forward to pour herself a glass of ice water from the pitcher.

"First off, I swear I didn't know about this when I invited you to my award's dinner."

She nodded as she took a sip, stealing a glance at Evan to see if he knew what was this about. He looked as confused as she felt.

"Since this award is another feather in Boston General's cap, the board thought it would be a good idea to host a luncheon for the staff, since obviously we can't invite them all to the ceremony."

"That is a nice idea. Shows you appreciate everyone's efforts to make the hospital what it is."

"What does that have to do with us?" Evan asked.

"I'd like you two to co-chair the committee to make that happen. We're on a time crunch, so I need you to get going right away. I figured you wouldn't mind working together during off-hours, since you're dating."

"Oh, we're not—" Hope looked nervously between Evan and Parker.

Evan, she noticed, remained silent.

"You're not?" Parker asked, looking Evan's way. "I thought, the ARF Gala ticket..."

"We *were* dating." Evan looked at her with a fake smile, then directed his attention back to their boss. "But apparently, we're not anymore."

Bitter much? And fuck off for telling Parker about them when that was expressly against the rules. The ire she'd had for James yesterday suddenly transferred to Evan.

"Well, that's too bad. I thought that would make it easier spending time together after hours. Anyway..." Parker launched into the day the board had in mind, the location, and the time.

"Wait. You mean, you still want us to work together on this?"

"Of course. You're both professionals, right?"

She was too mad at Evan to even want to look at him right now, let alone work with him.

"I don't think that's a good idea."

Parker's next move showed how he got his position as chief of staff.

He sighed. "You know, the board keeps talking about implementing a 'no fraternization' policy. I've assured them that is completely unnecessary. That my staff would have no problem working together, even if they broke up. Maybe I was wrong."

Hope thought about what a policy like that would mean for the employees at Boston General. Logistically, she knew they'd probably have to grandfather in current relationships and make exceptions for married couples, but still...

She put on her best fake smile and replied, "You're right. Of course, we can work on this together."

Well played, Parker.

"Great. I'd like you to get going on this right away. Feel free to use one of the conference rooms or the doctor's lounge if you need a neutral space."

She stood and glared at Evan; even madder now that her thoughts went to all the dirty things they'd done in her office. "That might be best."

Apparently, he either didn't notice her frosty attitude or was simply choosing to ignore it. "We could talk about first steps at lunch?"

At first, she was going to say fuck no, she didn't want to have lunch with him—in politer language, of course. Not only because she was pissed that he had a big mouth, but also being seen having lunch together would only fuel the rumor mill. But then she realized this would be the perfect alibi if Steven were to ask her about it. She could chalk it up to people trying to make something out of nothing.

"That should work." Her tone was all business. "I'll meet you in the cafeteria in an hour."

"I'll be there."

That almost sounded like a warning.

****

Evan

He had an idea about how to fix things with Hope.

"I'm going to talk to Steven," he said the minute she sat down across from him in the cafeteria booth.

"So?"

Hello, ice princess.

"So, I think if Steven understood my reasons, he might be willing to let bygones be bygones. And you and I can put this behind us."

"You can't just expect to explain to Steven and think everything will magically be fine. It doesn't work that way, Evan. You don't get to treat people like shit, then expect to be forgiven just because you say you're sorry."

"I know I'll have to make things right with your brother, and that may take time. But if he sees you're happy..."

"You took it upon yourself to tell people about us—without even talking to me. Thinking that everything would be fine because you're sorry for treating your friend bad and not talking to him about what was bothering you—like a friend should."

"I screwed up, Hope. I feel bad about it, but there's not much I can do other than try to fix it and move on. I don't know what you want from me."

"I don't want anything from you! I just wanted to keep things as they were, but you had to ruin that."

"If you think the idea of being my girlfriend is ruining things between us, then maybe you're right about seeing other people, because it's obvious we want different things out of this relationship."

"We don't have a relationship! That's what you're not getting. We had an agreement—rules—for a reason. So, we didn't develop feelings and complicate things."

"Hope, we had feelings for one another after the first night."

"Yeah, dislike."

"Bullshit. You know as well as I do that there's been something special between us from the beginning."

"We had amazing sexual chemistry, Evan. I'm not arguing that."

Had. Past tense.

"If you honestly think that's all there is between us, we might as well call it a day, because I don't think there's anything left to say."

"Well, then I guess that's it, then."

He pursed his lips and shook his head at her. "I guess so." He stood up with his tray. "I'll email you my ideas. We should be able to get this done electronically."

"Agreed."

He paused before walking away. "Take care of yourself, Hope Ericson."

Without another word, he turned on his heel and didn't look back.

Chapter Forty-Eight

Hope

She was glad she had her anger. It kept her from breaking down every time his name popped up on her email.

But at night when she lay awake in the quiet condo, his words kept coming back to her, and the tears would stream down her face.

"What about our babies? The ones we could have together."

"I don't want to see other people."

She didn't want him seeing other people, either. In fact, the mere idea of his hands on someone else made her nauseous.

Why are you upset? This is what you wanted!

But dating other people herself had no appeal. She'd almost thrown up in her mouth when she agreed to go to happy hour with Jay Johnson. The physical therapist was charming enough, but Hope got the impression that he was the type of guy who wouldn't think twice about canceling their date if something better came along.

Evan's words continued to play in her head. "If your brother sees you happy…"

Was that true? Would Steven not view her dating his nemesis as a slap in the face?

"I'll make things right with your brother."

Apparently, he no longer felt the need to since they were over, because Steven never mentioned a word about it when he asked her to dog sit Ralph and Lola that weekend while he and Whitney went on their bed-and-breakfast vacation.

"A little early to see the colors…" she'd remarked with a smirk. Francine had blabbed that she'd shipped their grandma's engagement ring to him.

"I don't care. We need to get away. So, do you think it'd be okay if Billy and Claire dropped them off on Friday?"

Okay, if he wasn't going to tell her, she'd play dumb.

"Sure. That's no problem. I'd love the company."

"Hey, speaking of company… I sponsored Parker's table at the Person of the Year ceremony. I hear he invited you."

"You sponsored his table? That was generous of you."

He shrugged. "I wanted to thank him for how supportive he was when Whitney lost the baby. And maybe butter him up in case I want to take more time off in the near future."

She was itching to ask what he would possibly need time off for, but decided if he'd wanted to tell her—he would have already.

"Smart. Although, I'm surprised he said yes. I would think he'd want to sit with the board."

"I think he agreed because he's bringing his girlfriend. We're a lot more fun than his usual crowd."

"I heard he was dating someone he met at the ARF Gala." She didn't reveal what else she knew about that night.

"He's not divulging much about her, but I've noticed he's no longer living at the hospital, so that's a good thing."

"Did he tell you Evan is also part of his table?"

Other than the clench of his jaw, he didn't respond to hearing Evan's name. "Yeah, he mentioned that."

"And you're okay with that?"

"I figured if I could be cordial when he came to the Cape, I can be cordial at a dinner."

Hmm. Interesting.

On Thursday, she sent Evan a text, not an email.

Hope: What's your schedule look like this week? I have a few things I wanted to run by you about the party favors and decorations for the luncheon, and it would be easier to explain in person.

He didn't respond for several hours. Finally…

Evan: We can meet in the conference room tomorrow around two.

Hope: I was thinking more like lunch?

Evan: I don't think that's a good idea.

Ouch.

Hope: Okay, see you at two in the conference room then.

He didn't reply.

****

Evan

It had killed him not to jump at the chance to have lunch with her. But he wasn't going to be her chump, either. She'd moved on—apparently, she had a hot date with Jay Johnson at Friday's happy hour.

Good luck getting that weasel to fuck you dirty, socialite.

Evan wasn't going to beg for her scraps. He was already pathetic enough sitting in his storage room, pulling her clothes from her boxes to smell, while he replayed their little rendezvous there in his head.

Like he said, pathetic.

He walked into the cafeteria the next day, looking for an empty chair, when a group of nurses summoned him over to their table. They were cute with bad reputations.

Why not? It was time he quit moping around.

Sitting down, he gave them his most charming smile. The one that always guaranteed to get a phone number slipped in his hand. The same one he'd used to get Hope to take him back to her office that first day.

Speaking of the socialite. She was walking his way with none other than the weasel himself. He was carrying one tray for the both of them. *How sweet.*

They sat down in a booth that was in his straight line of sight. He knew the second she noticed him because she flashed Jay her sexiest smile and made sure to reach across the table and touch his hand.

Two could play that game.

He threw his arm along the back of the booth, behind a blonde nurse's shoulders. Her name badge said *Glenda*.

"Are any of you ladies working tomorrow?"

"All three of us are," Jackie, the dark-haired nurse across the table, answered. "Are you?"

"I am. And I'm going to happy hour."

"What a coincidence," Glenda purred and placed her hand on his thigh. "I am, too."

Evan had to will himself not to move away from her touch. He knew Hope had a direct view of them and where the nurse's hand was.

He stared down at the woman like she was the most interesting woman in the world. "It must be my lucky day," he said and was rewarded with her giggling and twirling her hair.

"Must be."

"Well, ladies," he said, sliding out of the booth. "Duty calls." He winked at Glenda. "See you tomorrow."

The eruption of squeals reached his ears just as he walked by Hope and Jay, and he didn't even try to hide his smile.

****

Hope

She'd wanted to jump out of the booth and smack that nurse when she put her hand on Evan's thigh.

This is what you wanted.

No, it really wasn't. What she wanted was to have him all to herself while her brother never found out.

Fair? No.

Selfish? Yes.

The truth? As ugly as it was… yes. She wasn't proud of it.

Holding her notebook against her chest, she took a deep breath and blew it out before walking through the conference room door at three minutes to two.

It was empty, even though he'd left the cafeteria before she did.

She'd give him until ten after, and then she was leaving.

At eight minutes after two, a text came through.

Evan: Sorry, have to reschedule. Something came up.

Whatever.

Hope: Don't worry about it. I'll just go ahead with my plans as I see fit.

Evan: You can't just email me your ideas?

Hope: As I told you in an earlier text, it's too complicated to try to explain electronically.

Evan: I don't understand what could possibly be so complicated about some streamers and trinkets.

She pulled the socialite card that he was always accusing her of.

Hope: Of course, you wouldn't understand. Like I said, I'll take care of it. Your input isn't necessary; I was simply being courteous.

She deleted the middle finger emoji she'd added before she hit send.

Evan: Fine, I'll be there in five minutes.

Hope: Sorry. Already left. I have another meeting to go to.

She grabbed her notebook and high-tailed it out of there—going straight to the lab where she knew he wouldn't bother her.

Evan: You have another meeting? How is that possible when we had one scheduled?

Hope: Exactly. *Asshole.* Again, she deleted the profanity before she sent the message.

Evan: I work in an *emergency room,* Hope. Things happen.

She was going to have to call bullshit on that one.

Hope: If that were true, how could you all of a sudden breakaway?

Evan: Like I said, things happen.

Hope: Whatever. Email me the caterer's bid.

Evan: I thought you were handling the catering?

Hope: You better be kidding.

He sent her back a winking emoji.

Don't try to flirt with me, jerk. Save it for Glenda.

Of course, she didn't say that, just put her phone on silent and threw it in her purse.

There'd been no need to put it on silent—he never sent anything else.

She wasn't disappointed when she looked at her phone hours later. Not at all.

CHAPTER FORTY-NINE

Evan

He'd made it to happy hour. Yippee.

The minute that fucker Jay put his arm around Hope's waist as he handed her a glass of wine, Evan was seeing red.

The three naughty nurses were pawing at him like they were bears and he was dipped in honey. Apparently, word had spread about his threesome in the doctor's lounge last year. He should be all over this, but his attention was focused on the couple at the bar.

Evan recognized her smile was polite and not genuine when she talked to Jay. He also noticed she let him kiss her. Right fucking there for everyone to see.

Something Evan had wanted to do from the first night he'd met her. Only it was against her goddamn rules.

Apparently, the rules didn't apply to Jay Johnson.

Fuck it, they no longer applied to him, either.

"Ladies... what do you say we take this party elsewhere?"

****

Hope

She wanted to cry as she watched Evan slide out of his booth and wrap an arm around two of the three girls who'd been fawning over him since he walked in. They were the same nurses from yesterday in the cafeteria. The third woman practically skipped alongside them as they walked out the door.

She could envision all the dirty things they were going to do. The things he used to do with her. Things they'd promised they'd only do with each other.

That was before.

Everything was different now.

She tried to put on a happy face as Jay Johnson droned on about his time playing baseball at LSU. Who the hell cared?

"Personally, I'm a fan of University of Arizona baseball. Danny Roberts, my friend Danielle's dad, went there."

"Danny Roberts?" he said pompously. "Please. He didn't go to Arizona."

Uh, yeah, he did.

And she was done. Even with Evan leaving with the bimbos, she couldn't bring herself to want to spend any more time with this pompous guy. Not to mention, he kissed like a dead fish.

"I should get going. I have to let the dogs out."

"You have dogs?"

She didn't feel like explaining they were her brother and future sister-in-law's.

"Yep. Two of them. So, I need to go."

"You should have gone home to let them out before you came here. That was irresponsible of you as a pet owner."

Hope wasn't about to explain to this fool that they were walked that afternoon by their paid dogwalkers.

She slipped her purse over her shoulder as she stood. "You're right. Thanks for the drink. Have a nice night."

Then she went home and sobbed in the shower.

And in front of the TV as she ate ice cream out of the container.

The only time she got up the rest of the weekend was to let the dogs out and feed them, use the bathroom, and answer the door for her pizza and ice cream orders. Yes—orders, plural.

Yvette called Saturday night, but Hope didn't have the energy to tell her friend what had happened. She didn't want to relive it.

Especially when she acknowledged this was her doing. What did she expect when she told him they needed to see other people?

She didn't even know what day it was when, out of nowhere, Steven was standing in the living room, asking, "Are you sick? What's wrong?"

Where had he come from? She hadn't even heard him come in. Whitney stood next to him, her face full of concern as she looked at Hope laying on the couch—food containers strewn about. All the food was probably why Lola and Ralph hadn't left her side all weekend.

She opened her mouth to answer him but couldn't get the words out as a sob stuck in her throat and tears streamed down her face.

Lola let out a whine and laid her head on Hope's shoulder while Ralph pawed at her legs.

"What's wrong?" Steven asked again.

She was finally able to squeak out, "Nothing!" then rolled away from him. "I'll be fine. Just leave me be. Let me wallow in peace."

"Wallow? What are you wallowing about?"

She didn't answer him, just continued to quietly sob.

Surprisingly, he did as she asked and let her cry in peace.

CHAPTER FIFTY

Hope
She woke up on the couch, the dogs still sprawled on her. Early morning light was peeking through the window.

She had no idea what day it was. Her phone was dead, so that was no help.

Switching on the TV—Steven must have turned it off once she fell asleep—she turned to the guide to discover it was Monday morning.

Well, at least I didn't miss work.

Hope shut the television back off and stood, waking the dogs up in the process. They jumped off the couch and headed to the back door to be let out.

She obliged them, then plugged her phone in. Her phone buzzed with messages once it got enough of a charge. There were a few from Yvette, one from Steven telling her that he and Whitney went back to her brownstone and they'd pick the dogs up that morning, and one from her mom.

Nothing from Evan.

Not that she was expecting one. Probably after a night with the triplets, he'd forgotten all about her.

Screw him. Wallowing was over.

She cleaned up her mess in the living room, let the dogs in and fed them, then jumped in the shower and got ready for work.

Wearing her favorite Chanel suit that always made her feel like a boss bitch, Hope tossed her hair over her shoulder and walked out the front door, head held high.

Evan who?

****

Evan

He'd checked his phone all weekend; for what, he had no idea. Like she was going to text and ask, "So how was your night with the nurses?"

He'd even resorted to checking his email—even when he wasn't working. That's when he saw Parker's email last night requesting an update from him and Hope today at one o'clock. It was as good a reason as any to request a meeting with her, which he did—through email. Because he was a chickenshit like that.

She replied early Monday morning—much earlier than she normally checked her email. It was curt and to the point.

The conference room is booked. We can meet at eleven in the doctor's lounge.

He emailed back. **I'll be there**.

He'd had every intention of playing nice with her. Maybe even being contrite—which would be hard as fuck for him, but he'd do it for her. Then, as he walked toward the doctor's lounge for the meeting, he saw her in the hall talking to Francisco Valencia. And she gave the man her genuine smile.

Oh, hell no.

****

Hope

She sat at the table in the lounge area. The TV was blaring some noisy game show. It was next to the hall leading to the sleep pods, which seemed counter-productive. But she slept in her bed at night like a normal person, so what did she know? Maybe the pods were soundproof.

Glancing at her watch, she bit back her annoyance. It was five past eleven. Evan obviously had no respect for her time—or her, for that matter.

The door opened and in walked the giggling Glenda, with Evan right behind her—his arms wrapped around her waist as he murmured in her ear and directed her toward the pod hall.

He acted like he was surprised to see her.

"Oh, hey, Hope. That's right, we're supposed to meet. Can you, uh, come back in about fifteen—" He looked at Glenda and corrected himself, to the other woman's delight, based on her cackle. "Thirty minutes?"

"You're such an asshole, Evan," she whispered with tears in her eyes as she walked to the door and yanked it open.

She hadn't made it three steps when she felt him grab her elbow and turn her around.

"I thought you liked it when I'm an asshole, socialite?" he sneered.

Hope jabbed him in the chest with her index finger and hissed, "Don't you dare throw that in my face," as the tears fell down her cheeks.

Evan blanched and took a step back, but he didn't apologize. Far from it.

"This is what you wanted, isn't it? For us to be with other people?"

"Of course, it's not!" she blurted out without thinking.

He dragged his fingers through his hair, leaving it sticking up where he did. "Then why are you doing this, Hope?"

She noticed two people walking down the hall toward them and remained silent until they were out of sight.

"It's just better this way, Evan."

"Better for who? 'Cause it's sure as hell not better for me."

With a snort, she looked pointedly at the doctor's lounge where the nurse had yet to emerge from. She was probably waiting naked in one of the pods for him to come back. "Yeah, you seem to be suffering."

Evan took a step closer and grabbed her elbow. "Are you fucking for real? You think I was really going to sleep with her?"

She shrugged and yanked her elbow from his grip. "You looked like you were well on your way."

"And I suppose you think I'd forgotten all about you waiting for me."

"What if I hadn't been waiting, Evan? Are you saying you wouldn't have given in to your urges?"

"The only urges I have are for you. I saw you outside with Francisco, Hope. I already knew you were here."

"And what about Friday? With the triplets?" She hated herself for showing her vulnerability and revealing that she'd noticed.

"I didn't do anything with them. Once we reached the parking lot, I pretended to get called into work. Ask anyone—I was here all weekend."

"So, what, you wanted to hurt me?"

He looked at the ceiling and took a deep breath, as if asking for patience from above. "No, you dumb girl, I wanted to make you jealous."

Once again, her mouth was working before her brain had a chance to filter it. "Well, it worked."

His eyebrows shot up. Her admission seemed to surprise him as much as it had her.

Taking a tentative step closer, he put his hand gently on her hip and said softly. "Well, I'm glad."

"That I was jealous?"

"Yes. It means you still care about me."

"What are we doing, Evan?" she whispered—her eyes never leaving his. "This will never work."

"Bullshit, it has to." He stroked her tenderly above her waistband. "Because even though I've never experienced it before, I think we're in love."

Hope put her hand on his chest and moved her fingers in circles above his heart. "Not the L word. That should definitely be a rule."

He ran his fingertips along her jawline. "But it's not, socialite, and I'm afraid it's true." Then he dipped his face to kiss her.

His lips were warm and firm, and she found herself wrapping her arms around his neck as his tongue tangled with hers.

"Ahem."

They broke apart to find Parker standing in front of them with a scowl on his face.

"I—um," Hope started, but then realized she couldn't explain her way out of what her boss had just witnessed. "Hi, Dr. Preston."

"Ms. Ericson." He nodded curtly, then addressed Evan. "Dr. Lacroix."

"Parker."

He stared at them for a beat and Hope wondered what kind of trouble they'd just gotten themselves into. Although she hadn't seen anything in the hospital handbook, she assumed two employees making out in the hall on duty was frowned upon.

"It just came to my attention that you two may need some time off to plan the luncheon properly. I suggest you take the rest of the afternoon to... get things figured out."

She pressed her lips together to keep from smiling. Evan, however, was grinning from ear to ear when he replied, "That's exactly what we need."

"Use this time wisely," their boss warned.

Hope knew she was beaming when she responded, "Of course."

Parker gave a stern nod, but there was a twinkle in his eye that she'd noticed had been there a lot lately—ever since the ARF Gala. There'd even been rumors that he wasn't working seven days a week anymore.

"Get out of here before I change my mind," he snarled.

"You got it." Evan grabbed her hand and pulled her down the hall, not letting go until he opened the passenger door to his Mercedes in the parking garage.

"Where are we going?" she asked when he slid behind the wheel.

"Wherever you want. I don't care, as long as you're with me."

"So cheesy."

He started the car and put it into drive. "Whatever. But you loved it, and you know it."

"Maybe. The jury's still out."

He glanced at her as he maneuvered his car toward the exit. "It is? Why? What are you waiting for?"

She shrugged. "Things."

A knowing grin crept up along his face, and he grabbed her hand to bring her knuckles to his lips. "Don't worry, socialite. After I make love you to you, I promise I'll still pull your hair and fuck your ass, too."

"Okay," she confessed with a smirk. "I loved it. Now, where are we going?"

"How about... our place."

Hope jerked her hand from his. "Slow down, Dr. Love. I'm not moving in with you."

He lifted one shoulder. "You also said you weren't going to fall in love with me, yet here we are. Although to be fair, you haven't actually admitted it."

"Maybe I don't."

"You do."

She leaned her head back against the headrest and watched as he drove through afternoon traffic with ease. He was always in control. It was so damn sexy.

"I do," she admitted with a sigh.

"I know."

She playfully slapped his arm. "You're such an arrogant ass."

Evan captured her hand and kissed it again. "I know that, too. I also know it's part of the reason you love me."

"You're not wrong. But I'm in therapy, so..."

His laugh rang through the car's cabin. "I'm afraid there's no cure for me, baby, other than to marry me, have my babies, and grow old with me."

"Oh. My. God. You really need to pump your brakes."

"Fine. But just know, it's going to happen. Sooner rather than later."

She couldn't think of anything she wanted more.

Epilogue

Hope

"I had an interesting conversation with your brother this morning," Evan announced as he stood in her office doorway.

"Oh boy." She'd had a feeling this was coming. "What happened?" Hope gave him the once-over as he sat down. "I don't see any bruises or scraped knuckles, so it must not have been that bad."

"Well, at first I thought he was going to deck me for breaking his little sister's heart."

She gasped. "He knew?"

"He knew. What surprised him was when I told him *you* dumped *me*—since apparently you were a blubbering mess when he got home Sunday night, after getting engaged. You kind of killed the happy couple's mood with your sobbing."

Hope put her head on her desk. "Oh god. I feel terrible." But she lifted her head with a smile. "So, he asked her. I'm so happy for them."

"Yeah, we're having dinner with them tonight to celebrate."

"Wait—what?" What alternate universe had she wandered into?

"I laid it out for him—all of it. That I'd thought he was Olivia's baby daddy, that we've been seeing each other pretty much since the night of the train accident, that I'm in love with you..."

"You didn't! What did he say?"

"He made me feel like a dick for not talking to him about Olivia and jumping to conclusions."

"Which you deserve," she interjected.

He nodded. "Which I deserved. I apologized, told him I would take good care of you, we bro-hugged, and then made dinner plans for tonight."

"Guys are so weird."

"He did promise to cut my balls off if I hurt you, if that makes you feel any better."

"A little."

Her phone rang. It was Yvette.

"I need to take this. I kind of ignored her calls this weekend while I was being a blubbering mess."

"Okay." He stood to walk out but paused in the doorway. "Dinner's at Chez Magnifique at seven. I'll pick you up at six thirty. Bring an overnight bag."

"Sounds good," she told him with a wave at the same time she clicked the answer button. "Hi! I'm so sorry I didn't call you back this weekend. I was in crisis, but everything's fine now."

Better to start off with an apology. Her friend was owed that—it'd been shitty to ignore her calls.

"Well, that makes two of us that were in crisis. Except, everything is not fine here."

Hope switched ears. "What's going on?"

"Do you still want to go into partnership with me on a bed-and-breakfast?"

She jolted forward. "Yes! Of course! I would love to! Why? Did you lose your job?"

"No, I quit. I'm pregnant."

****

Get James and Yvette's story in *Wicked Hot Baby Daddy*, available now!

https://books2read.com/wickedbabydaddy

Wicked Hot Doctor—Steven and Whitney's book, is available now! Get it here:

https://tesssummersauthor.com/wicked-hot-doctor-1

Wicked Bad Decisions, Zach and Zoe's story, coming May 31, 2022.

https://books2read.com/wickeddecisions

Wicked Dirty Secret, Olivia's story, will be available in July 2022.

Sign up for my newsletter to be the first to receive the bonus scene from the storeroom when it's ready!

https://www.subscribepage.com/TessSummersNewsletter

WICKED HOT BABY DADDY

The player doctor left behind more than a broken heart.

Dr. James Rudolf made Yvette Sinclair believe in fairytales, and he was her Prince Charming. Then out of the blue, he stopped taking her calls. Blocked them would be a more accurate descriptor.

Devastated, Yvette had no idea why the man she thought was *the one* had ghosted her. Even harder, she was three thousand miles away, so she couldn't just show up at his house and demand an explanation. Then her best friend started seeing him around Boston—a different beautiful woman on his arm each time. She felt like such a fool.

She was determined to move on and forget all about the playboy. Until two pink lines made that impossible.

https://tesssummersauthor.com/wicked-hot-baby-daddy

WICKED HOT SILVER FOX

It all started with a dirty photo in his text messages…

Yeah, Dr. Parker Preston's intentions when he gave Alexandra Collins his phone number at the animal rescue gala were more personal than professional. But he'd never expected the sassy beauty with the blue streak in her hair to send him a picture of her perfect, perky boobs as enticement to adopt the dogs she was desperately trying to find a home for.

But, dang if they weren't the ideal incentive for him to offer his home to more than just the dogs. In exchange for adopting the older, bonded pair, she'd need to move in with him for a month and get the dogs acclimated. Oh, and she wouldn't be sleeping in the guest room during her stay.

The deal is only for a month though. And she insisted they weren't going to fall in love, something he readily agreed with. They had the rules in place, what could possibly go wrong in four short weeks?

Get it here! https://tesssummersauthor.com/wicked-hot-silver-fox-1

WICKED HOT DOCTOR

A single doctor and a single lawyer walk into a bar…

Dr. Steven Ericson never thought a parking ticket would change his life, but that's exactly what happened the day he goes downtown to pay his forgotten ticket for an expired meter.

As the head of Boston General's ER, he doesn't have time for relationships, or at least he's never met a woman who made him want to make time.

That all changes when he meets Whitney Hayes. The dynamo attorney in high heels entices him to imagine carving out time for more than his usual one-night stand. Imagine his dismay to find out that she, too, doesn't do relationships—they're not in her 5-year plan.

Yeah, eff that. Her plan needs rewriting, and Steven's more than willing to supply the pen and ink to help with that.

https://tesssummersauthor.com/wicked-hot-doctor-1

THANK YOU

Thank you for reading *Wicked Hot Medicine!*

I'm so excited to bring you this series. I feel like I can't write the stories fast enough! After Yvette and James, and Olivia and her mystery man, (**edited to add, Zach and Zoe are cutting in line… they have been chattering in my ear.) I'm planning on bringing you Zach and Zoe, Aiden and Dakota, Liam and Utah, and of course, the dogwalkers, Billy and Claire.

If you enjoyed the book (and even if you didn't), would you mind leaving me a review on Amazon and/or Goodreads (and Bookbub if it's not too much trouble)? Believe it or not, your review does help get my book seen by other readers, which lets me keep writing.

Don't forget to sign up for my newsletter to get free bonus content and be the first to know about cover reveals, contests, excerpts, and more!

https://www.subscribepage.com/TessSummersNewsletter

xoxo,

Tess

ACKNOWLEDGMENTS

Mr. Summers: Thanks for being the best newsletter proofer a girl could ask for, and for putting up with me when I'm a hot mess trying to meet a deadline. And for kissing my neck when I'm trying to work. (I secretly love it.)

Marla Selkow Esposito: Thank you for making this book better and for being patient when I squeaked it in a few minutes past midnight.

OliviaProDesigns: Thanks for another great cover. I love it.

Alyssa Faye and Truly Trendy PR: Thank you for freeing up my time to write all the words.

Renee Rose and Misty Malloy: I couldn't ask for more supportive people in my corner. Thank you.

Everyone at Tess Summers' Playhouse: You guys are awesome. Thanks for never failing to make my day brighter.

To my readers: You continue to humble and amaze me with your support, and I thank you from the bottom of my heart for letting me continue to bring you my stories.

SAN DIEGO SOCIAL SCENE

Operation Sex Kitten: **(Ava and Travis)**
https://books2read.com/u/3yzyG6?affiliate=off

The General's Desire: **(Brenna and Ron)**
https://books2read.com/u/m2Mpek?affiliate=off

Playing Dirty: **(Cassie and Luke)**
https://books2read.com/u/3RNEdj?affiliate=off

Cinderella and the Marine: **(Cooper and Katie)**
https://books2read.com/u/3LYenM?affiliate=off

The Heiress and the Mechanic: **(Harper and Ben)**
https://books2read.com/u/bQVEn6?affiliate=off

Burning Her Resolve: **(Grace and Ryan)**
https://books2read.com/u/bzoEXz?affiliate=off

This Is It: **(Paige and Grant)**
https://books2read.com/ThisIsIt?affiliate=off

AGENTS OF ENSENADA

Ignition: (Kennedy and Dante)
https://books2read.com/u/47leJa?affiliate=off
Inferno: (Kennedy and Dante)
https://books2read.com/u/bpaYGJ?affiliate=off
Combustion: (Reagan and Mason)
https://books2read.com/u/baaME6?affiliate=off
Reignited: (Taren and Jacob)
https://books2read.com/u/3ya2Jl?affiliate=off
Flashpoint: (Sophia and Ramon)
https://books2read.com/TessSummersFlashpoint?affiliate=off

About the Author

Tess Summers is a former businesswoman and teacher who always loved writing but never seemed to have time to sit down and write a short story, let alone a novel. Now battling MS, her life changed dramatically, and she has finally slowed down enough to start writing all the stories she's been wanting to tell, including the fun and sexy ones!

Married over twenty-six years with three grown children, Tess is a former dog foster mom who ended up failing and adopting them instead. She and her husband (and their three dogs) split their time between the desert of Arizona and the lakes of Michigan, so she's always in a climate that's not too hot and not too cold, but just right!

Contact Me!

Sign up for my newsletter: BookHip.com/SNGBXD
Email: TessSummersAuthor@yahoo.com
Visit my website: www.TessSummersAuthor.com
Facebook: http://facebook.com/TessSummersAuthor
TikTok: https://www.tiktok.com/@tesssummersauthor
Instagram: https://www.instagram.com/tesssummers/
Amazon: https://amzn.to/2MHHhdK
BookBub https://www.bookbub.com/profile/tess-summers
Goodreads - https://www.goodreads.com/TessSummers

Printed in Great Britain
by Amazon